THE GOSPEL ACCORDING
TO THE SON

ALSO BY NORMAN MAILER

THE GOSPEL ACCORDING TO THE SON

NORMAN MAILER

LITTLE, BROWN AND COMPANY

A *Little, Brown* Book

First published in the USA in 1997 by Random House

First published in Great Britain in 1997 by Little, Brown and Company

Copyright © 1997 by Norman Mailer

A CIP catalogue record for this book
is available from the British Library.

ISBN 0 316 64168 5

Printed and bound in Great Britain by Clays Ltd, St Ives plc

Little, Brown and Company (UK)
Brettenham House
Lancaster Place
London WC2E 7EN

*To Susan, Danielle, Elizabeth, Kate, Michael, Stephen,
Maggie, Matthew, and John Buffalo*

THE GOSPEL ACCORDING
TO THE SON

1

In those days, I was the one who came down from Nazareth to be baptized by John in the River Jordan. And the Gospel of Mark would declare that on my immersion, the heavens opened and I saw "a spirit like a dove descending." A mighty voice said: "You are My beloved Son in whom I am well pleased." Then the Spirit drove me into the wilderness, and I was there for forty days and was tempted by Satan.

While I would not say that Mark's gospel is false, it has much exaggeration. And I would offer less for Matthew, and for Luke and John, who gave me words I never uttered and described me as gentle when I was pale with rage. Their words were written many years after I was gone and only repeat what old men told them. Very old men. Such tales are to be leaned upon no more than a bush that tears free from its roots and blows about in the wind.

So I will give my own account. For those who would ask how my words have come to this page, I would tell them to look upon it as a small miracle. (My gospel, after all, will speak of miracles.) Yet I would hope to remain closer to the truth. Mark, Matthew, Luke, and John were seeking to enlarge their fold. And the same is true of other gospels written by other men. Some of these scribes would speak only to Jews who were ready to follow me after my death, and some preached only to gentiles who hated Jews but had faith in me. Since each looked to give strength to his own church, how could he not fail to mix what was true into all that was not? But then from all these churches one prevailed, and it chose but four gospels, condemning the others for placing "immaculate and sacred words" next to "shameless lies."

It is also true that whether four gospels had been favored or forty, no number would suffice. For where the truth is with us in one place, it is buried in another. What is for me to tell remains neither a simple story nor without surprise, but it is true, at least to all that I recall.

2

For fourteen years I was an apprentice, as were ten others, to Joseph the carpenter, and our first work as novices was to split logs. With the head of an ax we would drive a wedge forward until it divided the trunk along its length. Then we would split the trunk again, and still again, until many rough planks were obtained. And it took a good apprentice to guide the wedge, after which our boards were shaped by much trimming.

Nor was it easy to find communion with the wood. None of us could forget that apples from the tree in Eden had possessed knowledge of good and evil; sometimes it would seem that good and evil were still in the wood. A fine piece worked upon for days might betray your tool at the smallest mistake, and often the board seemed to split by itself. I came to believe that even a crude plank could act with knowledge of good and evil (and much desire to do the latter). But then, an evil man cannot pass by a fine tree without saddening its leaves.

Still, there was wisdom to be found in doing good work. When the task went well, I was at peace. The scent of a well-made chest cheered me, and I could feel a fine spirit between the grain and my hand. I do not know how else to say it. In my family we did not speak of such matters. Being Essenes we were, of all Jews, strictest in our worship of the one God and were full of scorn for Roman religions with their belief in many deities. So I could hardly talk to my family of a spirit in the wood. That was pagan, and I had been raised to be as devout as the husband of my mother, Joseph the carpenter. He wore white robes when he was not working, and washed them frequently, even when our well was low. Every Essene was supposed to strive for such cleanliness.

Therefore, we seldom married, and a man only lay with his wife when God told him to make a child. Jews who were not Essenes spoke of us as a sect that would die out (and soon!) unless we could make converts.

It will be understood, then: I was taught not to pursue

women or even to approach them. We were to live as warriors for the Lord. We were not to lie down with women when such acts could weaken our purpose. To live by this rule was law, even if the war would last for the length of one's life.

3

At the age of twenty-seven I finished my apprenticeship and became a master, but still worked with Joseph. In my youth, other apprentices had been jealous of me because they looked upon him as my father, but I could have told them that Joseph served God by treating all of his workers with as much respect as he gave to his work. When I was scrupulous in my labors, Joseph would nod and say, "You would make a good carpenter if God had wanted you to be one." What did Joseph mean? As he said such things, he would turn his head away as though to press his lips upon a secret.

Being old, his memory was weak, and he could not recall that he had told me this secret, the true story of my birth, when I was twelve. Yet I remembered even less, for he had related these events to me on our journey back to Nazareth from the Great Temple in Jerusalem, and what I learned was so far from the understanding of a boy that soon after our return, I fell into a long fever. All that Joseph told me seemed lost. Still, I do not think it was the fever that made me forget, but rather that I did not wish to remember. It was only after eighteen years had passed and I was thirty and mourning Joseph's death that I could recall what he told me when I was twelve.

In those years my family, together with other Essenes from Nazareth, rich and poor, would walk to Jerusalem in the week before Passover, all of us dressed in white, and we traveled in such numbers that we did not fear thieves on the road. The journey took three days from dawn to dark over the hills and valleys and deserts between Nazareth and Jerusalem, but after my twelfth year, however, they never went again.

For on that visit, even as they passed through the last gate of Jerusalem on their way home, I slipped out of the procession and ran all the way back to the Great Temple. Because all the children from Nazareth had stayed together, my mother did not notice my absence until later that morning.

When they didn't find me among friends, kinfolk, or neighbors, Mary and Joseph hastened back to the Great

Temple, and there they found me in one of the courtyards, with a number of priests and doctors. To the astonishment of my parents, I not only sat comfortably among these wise men but was speaking with them.

According to Joseph and Mary, my words were worthy of a prophet: a miracle.

Later, after the death of Joseph, I came to believe that I must preach and asked my mother what I had said on that day in the Temple eighteen years ago. But she would tell me no more than that my words were so holy she could not repeat them, no more than she could speak the name of the Lord aloud. Yet even as she refused, so did a better memory of that moment come back to me, and I, too, was delighted with my wisdom.

What, then, had I been saying? My spoken thoughts were not holy so much as difficult to comprehend. For in those years wise men in the synagogue often had learned discussions with each other about the Word. Had the Word always been with God?

Later, the Gospel of John commenced by saying: "In the beginning was the Word, and the Word was with God, and the Word was God." But that was written many years after I was gone. When I was twelve, the question was still in dispute. Had God made our flesh to be like the flesh of animals, or had He created us by His utterance alone?

Now, I could recall telling these learned elders that the Word had lived first in water even as the breath that carries our speech comes forth from our mouths in a cloud on a cold winter morning. Yet clouds also bring rain, I had said, and so the Word lives in the water of our breath. Thereby we belong to God. For all the waters, we know, are His, even as all the rivers go down to the sea.

In that hour, the priests told my mother, "Never in one so young have we heard such wisdom," and I would suppose that this praise decided Joseph to tell me the story of my birth in the course of our return to Nazareth.

What I now relate is how the story came back to me in my thirtieth year while praying at Joseph's funeral. Indeed, even as I prayed, I could still see the strain on his face on the day he told me that he was not my father.

4

Before I was born, Joseph had been a widower. He was many years older than my mother, but asked her to consider marriage. Since he was an Essene, he declared that he would respect their difference in age: To protect her, he would serve first as her guardian and then they would be wed. She agreed. And Joseph waited.

There came a night, however, when the angel Gabriel entered her bedchamber. As Mary would tell it to Joseph, this angel said: "The Lord is with thee. Blessed art thou among women."

My mother, like Joseph, was an Essene, and so was her mother. Virtue had built a fence around the first fence in order to guard her. Nonetheless, the angel Gabriel was radiant, and the white of his garment was like the light of the moon. In that light she shivered yet felt much admired. She also felt weak. All that she knew had left her.

The angel said, "Mary, thou hast found favor with God. Thou shalt conceive in thy womb and bring forth a son. Call his name Jesus. He shall be great and he shall be called the Son of the Highest." These words are taken from the Gospel of Luke, but according to my mother, the angel said little. All the same, she had seen the glory of the Lord (if only for an instant), and knew by the heavenly turn in her breast that she was with child. The scent of the air was sweeter than any garden. Then the angel left. He had not even touched her hand.

When Joseph learned that she was pregnant, he threw himself down and wept. "What prayer can be said," he asked, "on her behalf or on mine? She was a virgin and I did not protect her."

But then Joseph grew angry and said, "Why did you bring this shame on yourself?"

She began to cry. "I am innocent," she told him, "and I have never known a man."

Joseph did not know what to do. To conceal her sin would be to trespass upon the Law. Yet if he told the Essene priests, Mary could be stoned to death. He said to himself: "In quiet, I will put her away from me."

So Joseph made plans to hide her among relatives who

lived in the hills to the west. Mary, however, went to visit her own cousin, Elizabeth, who lived in the hills to the east, for Elizabeth was six months pregnant. And while Mary was gone, a voice came to Joseph in his sleep: "Take the young woman as your wife. For she is not pregnant by a man, and her son is blessed."

When Joseph awoke, it was with the conviction that they must wed. As soon as Mary returned to Nazareth, he married her, but he was scrupulous. Joseph did not know her, nor did he desire to know her until I was born. And they named me Jesus, which in Nazareth, by our rough dialect, is Yeshua. That was still my name when I went to visit John the Baptist and was blessed by him and spent forty days on a mountain in the wilderness. Before we can speak of those days, however, there is much to tell, and some of it is before my birth.

5

Joseph was proud of his ancestors; he could claim that he was descended from King David, who was father to King Solomon. For this reason Joseph wished his wife to bear her child in Bethlehem, since that is the city where King David was born, and where Joseph was born.

Mary was now heavy with me but willing to travel for three days from Nazareth to Bethlehem; she was proud of Joseph's ancestry. This is the truth of why we took that journey, and it is also true that I was born in a manger by the light of a candle. As all know by now, there was no room at the inn.

A few shepherds were guarding their flocks in the fields

surrounding us, and they came upon the manger soon after my birth. An angel appeared to them and pointed to the barn, and the angel said: "This day is born Christ, the Messiah of the Lord."

The shepherds told so many men and women about the angel that word soon came to Herod, the king of Israel, that there had been a holy birth in Bethlehem. Herod saw at once that any babe who had been watched over by an angel could yet become a king. He had no need of other kings.

6

By the year of my birth, Herod was old. People could no longer speak of him as the greatest warrior in Israel. But when he was young, his triumphs had been so many that he was full of lust and took ten wives.

The people of Israel did not love him. He was an Idumean from south of Judea, a Jew only in name, in truth a pagan. Caesar had made him emperor over all the Hebrews by declaration from Rome, and Herod put graven images of the Roman eagle on the gates of the Great Temple, a sacrilege forbidden by the Commandments. And his life was full of many unclean hours and evil deeds. Afflicted by suspicion, he could not trust the fidelity of his wife, Mariamne, his most beloved, and having convinced himself that she would soon betray him, he ordered his body-servant to slay her. Afterward he mourned Mariamne and gave large favors to the two sons he had had with her, but neither could forgive him. They sought to murder their father for the slaughter of their mother. They laid plots. They were discovered. They were beheaded. In Rome, Emperor Augustus said: "Better to be Herod's swine than his son." That was much repeated among the Jews.

Later, as Herod grew older, he grew mad. Not a day after he heard of my birth, he sent three wise men to Bethlehem. He said: "Find the holy babe and bring me word. I wish to come and worship." They did not believe him, but they knew they had to leave at once, and at night.

On the short journey to Bethlehem, a star came from the east and passed above them, then moved to the south, and they followed the star until they came to our manger. There, they knelt before Mary and Joseph, and gave worship. So it is told in the Gospel of Matthew. Matthew would also claim that the wise men brought gifts of gold and frankincense and myrrh—but that may not be true. For Joseph and Mary never spoke of such presents.

It is true, however, that the wise men offered one gift of considerable value: They warned Joseph not to live for even one more day under the rule of Herod. Indeed, these wise men were also quick to leave the land of Israel, and departed soon after they came to the manger. And Joseph left in the next hour. All of us traveled by night until we came to Egypt.

Herod exacted a vengeance. When the wise men did not return, executioners were sent to Bethlehem with a command to slay all male children who had been born at the time of my birth. The words of the prophet Jeremiah were fulfilled: "Lamentation and weeping and mourning."

Herod soon died, and Joseph came back to Nazareth, where he gave two sons to my mother, James and John. It may be that our love for each other was cursed, for in later years I did not feel as near to these brothers as to the children who had been slain in Bethlehem. When Joseph's death opened the seal of my mind, I brooded often upon those children and the life they never had.

7

Let it be understood that I was not unprepared to speak to the priests of the Great Temple. Like other children, I had started school before the age of five, and in our small synagogue we studied every day until nightfall. By the age of eight, I could even read the language of the old Israelites, and I knew the Commandments, which came down from Moses, and the laws derived from the Commandments. Since each law gave birth to ten laws, and each of these to another ten, there were now ten hundred laws concerning prayer and diet and the rules of sacrifice on the altar. And we also studied Genesis, Exodus, Leviticus, Numbers, and the book of Deuteronomy.

We read the prophecies of Elijah, and of Elisha and Ezekiel and Isaiah, and much of what was not in our few scrolls was remembered by our elders and teachers, who passed it on to us.

Yet on our return to Nazareth following our visit to the Great Temple in my twelfth year, I decided that if I had been given wisdom enough to speak to the wise men, that must have come from the spirits of those infants who were killed because of my birth.

An even greater weight was upon me. That was Joseph's story concerning my true father. I could hardly see myself as the Son. After school, on days when we would scuffle with each other, I would lose such fights as often as I won. How, then, could I be the Son of the Lord? And this doubt left me in fear of His wrath. For I remembered that the Lord had said to Moses, "Behold, these people will forsake Me and break My covenant and then shall My anger be kindled against them. They shall be burnt with hunger and devoured with burning heat . . ." And indeed the Lord's wrath may have been upon me as a result of having such thoughts. The great fever burned in my flesh soon after. In my twelfth year, I was all but devoured by that fever.

When I recovered, I had lost all memory of what Joseph had told me and was again like others, and even a young man, for now I was thirteen. I began my labors as an apprentice in Joseph's shop and spent seven years as a simple apprentice and seven again as a full apprentice before I became a young master.

The first seven years were spent in learning how to make mud-bricks for walls and put up framing for roofs and doors and windows. And I also acquired the skill to build beds and tables, stools and cabinets, boxes of all sizes, and plows and yokes for oxen. In my second apprenticeship I worked, however, in Sepphoris, the capital of Galilee, an hour on foot from Nazareth. There I learned more of my craft by working in fine houses, and Joseph taught us much, for he knew many arts.

Here too lived Herod Antipas, the son of Herod, and this Herod Antipas had become king of Galilee, Idumea, and Judea. When I would watch him pass in procession, I did not know why my blood raced like a steed and I was ready to bolt. My heart was speaking to me even if my mind was not; I had no sense of why I should feel such fear at the sight of King Herod Antipas taking his royal passage through the avenues of Sepphoris. All I knew was that I seemed to have no greater wish afterward than to propitiate all bad feelings (and good ones) by working with care. My life was devoted to the practice of carpentry.

8

Joseph used to say: "Where one plank is joined to another by a man who cares for the subtlety of the joint, the first piece will cleave to the second as in a marriage that is blessed. But boards joined by nails fall apart when the nail rusts; so, too, is marriage corroded by adultery."

I do not know if it was for such a reason, but none of us were given iron implements until after we had served our first seven years with tools of bronze. Joseph would often speak of the trials of carpenters from ancient times and other lands: He would tell how the Egyptians fashioned small chests of much delicacy out of no better wood than acacia, sycamore, or tamarisk. Such grains were fibrous and often knotty, and each surface had to be finished with paint and gold leaf. Yet this work of the Egyptians, although limited by their bronze tools, had proved more beautiful than our own, and Joseph even owned a small Egyptian chest whose dovetailed corners were a wonder to him.

When we began to use iron tools, it was with caution, even fear. We all knew the visions of Daniel and how the teeth of the fourth beast are iron and terrible in their strength.

All the same, I learned. After a time, I could make good use of iron, and was able to work my tools upon woods from many lands: maple, beech, oak, yew, fir, lime, and cedar. Oak we would select as framing for a door, and maple, which was supple, for beds, keeping cedar, which was sweet-smelling, for chests. Wild olive, being very hard, was for tool handles.

I had friends in other workshops who could plate metal objects in gold and silver; some of us even spoke of traveling from Sepphoris to Rome so we might apprentice our skills to great masters. But this was no more than talk; we never failed to observe our daily acts of purity. And we knew that Rome was full of license. It was said that the emperor and empress indulged in lewd acts of which you would not wish to speak for fear that a vile sore might visit your tongue.

So my trade became my pride, and I knew respect for

the tools in my box. A rasp, a plane, a hammer, an auger, a gimlet, an adze, a cubit rule, a saw, and three chisels for paring, as well as a gouge—all were mine. And my knowledge of how to treat wood became another tool.

When we used fir for flooring, we offered prayers that it not burn. For fire seemed attracted to fir. And other prayers were said over winter oak, which was liable to decay. Cypress was blessed; it resisted the worm.

Joseph also taught many ways to put up walls of stone for large buildings, and told us of a substance called pozzolana, an earth that came from the volcanoes south of Rome; this pozzolana, mixed with lime, became a cement. Such knowledge led me to think of the wisdom of the Lord, who knew the earth so well that heavy soil thrown far from its home by a volcano could find a new nature for itself and hold loose stones together. Often would I ponder on the substances of His Kingdom that we worked upon with our hands.

9

Living with such skills, I was at peace. But rare is the calm that is long free of disturbance. Even as Joseph was in his last days I began to dream of the Great Temple in Jerusalem, and I wondered if it was too late for me to learn how to cast in gold and silver. Thoughts came to me that I would yet work upon the Holy Altar, but I distrusted them, for they left me full of a greed that was stifling to the throat; I had to wonder whether it was wise for a modest man to work with gold. All the same, I was ready. And for what, I did not know. I felt as if I were a man enclosing another man within.

Joseph died, and I mourned him. Soon I was distraught. His great secret came back to me. If I knew again that the Lord was my Father, I hardly knew in what manner, He was still far from me. Whenever I thought that He would soon appear, He did not. I was in need of new wisdom.

It was then I decided to make a pilgrimage to that prophet and holy man who was John the Baptist, and indeed, I could even say that I knew him before I saw him, since he was my cousin. I had heard my mother speak often and well of John, even if others did not. He was held in ill repute among the Pharisees in our synagogue. These Pharisees of Nazareth were, in the main, devout, although never equal in piety to us; being merchants, they grew fat, but then they had many appetites, and not all were clean. No matter—they spoke of John as if he were a wild creature. All the same, I felt close to my cousin. I did not know him, yet he was kin to me. Much was alike in the way we were conceived.

His father, Zacharias, had been an Essene priest; his mother was the same Elizabeth whom my mother had visited when pregnant with me, and Elizabeth was most devout and was as thin as a tall blade of grass. So, too, was Zacharias; they believed that the body must be kept as a temple. Only a pure body could offer pure prayers in the struggle against the powers of evil.

Therefore, they remained childless. And were happy. But there came a time when Elizabeth began to mourn that she was barren. One day she even prayed for a child. And her prayer was heard. That morning, as Zacharias stood alone at the altar performing a priest's office, an angel came to him. (Indeed, this angel was the same Gabriel who would in six months speak to my mother.)

Gabriel said: "Zacharias, do not tremble. I bring good news. Elizabeth shall bear a son."

Now, Zacharias was not at ease. No angel had ever appeared to him before. So he said: "I am an old man, and my wife is close to me in age. Who can you be?" Whereupon the angel grew angry. "Since you do not believe me," he said, "you will not speak until the day that Elizabeth gives birth." And when Zacharias came out of the synagogue, he was dumb. Nothing could be heard but the straining of his throat.

He returned to his house and was silent. Yet soon enough he would marvel. For on this same day that he lost his speech, he was able to rise and give issue to Elizabeth. And she conceived. Soon, she was so afraid she might lose what had been given her that she remained in bed. And the unborn child did not stir.

In the sixth month of this pregnancy, Gabriel visited my mother. Afterward, even as Joseph was wondering how to serve as her guardian, Mary went into the high hills to visit her cousin.

And in the moment that Elizabeth saw my mother at the door, so did her babe leap in her womb. Overjoyed, she spoke out: "Blessed art thou, Mary. All generations to come shall call you blessed."

Mary felt honored by these words. Elizabeth's ancestry (on the side not related to my mother) was said to go back as far as Aaron, the brother of Moses. Elizabeth's blessing stayed in my mother's ear, and her pride became as great as her humility. Few could contradict her will. My mother would say: "He that is mighty has done to me great things." It soon became her belief that all she said could only be the truth. She would speak often and fondly of John the Baptist. "Only when Elizabeth saw me," she liked to say, "was John able to quicken in the womb."

And on the day my cousin was born the tongue of Zacharias grew loose, and he spoke, and could bless his son.

John grew up. He was lean, more lean even than Zacharias or Elizabeth, and he lived alone in the desert. He preached near a ford in the River Jordan, and pilgrims came to him in great fear of their sins. He preached with such force of word and spirit that the High Priest of the Great Temple sent Levites out from Jerusalem, and they asked: "Who art thou? Art thou the Christ?"—Christ being the word for Messiah in Greek, a language that many of the elevated in Jerusalem liked to use.

But John said, "I baptize with water, no more. I am not the Messiah." These Pharisees were dissatisfied. They said: "You perform baptisms yet you are not Christ. Who are you, then?"

"I am the voice of one crying in the wilderness," John replied. "But there is one coming after me whom you do not know. He is chosen above me by the Lord, and I am not worthy to loosen the straps of his sandals." And John said it on the day before I went to visit him, although I had no idea that he spoke of such things. I had thought to go as one more pilgrim.

10

People said, and it was true when I saw him, that the Baptist wore but one small wrapping of camel's hide to conceal his loins. He was so naked to the sun that he looked darker than any of his visitors, a thin man with a thin beard.

I had also heard how he believed that meat and wine inspire demons to live in one's body; therefore he ate nothing but wild honey and locusts, the poorest food of the poor. Yet it was said that these locusts could devour all the disbelief in the hearts of those who came to John. And the wild honey gave warmth to his voice when he spoke in the words of Isaiah: "'The crooked shall be made straight and the rough ways made smooth.'"

Yet I had also been told that the locusts he ate kept him harsh in spirit and he would greet penitents by saying: "Generation of vipers, who has warned you to flee from the wrath to come?"

The people would ask: "What shall we do?" And John the Baptist would answer: "Let him who has two coats give one to the man who has none." And he would always speak of the man mightier than himself who was yet to come.

Yet when I first saw his face, I wished to hide my own. For I knew that he would not be long among us. And I knew this as if I heard a beating of wings overhead.

I had joined a group of many people and so I could stare at John before he saw me and was able to watch the pilgrims as they were baptized and departed. I remained. Even in the loneliness of this place in the desert, he still could not see me, for I concealed myself in the shadow of a rock. It was only when the others were gone and the stones were hot from the sun that I came forward. To which he said, "I have waited for you."

His eyes had more light than the sky, yet they were paler than the moon. His thin beard was long. The hair that grew from his ears was matted, and so too was the hair that grew from his cheeks. A wing and a leg of a locust were caught in his beard. I wondered how this man who bathed others and washed himself many times a day could still show such leavings. Yet it was not unfitting. His face was like a ravine and small creatures would live within.

Looking at me, he said, "You are my cousin." Then he said, "I knew that you would come today."

"How can you know?"

He sighed. His breath was as lonely as the wind that passes through empty places. He said, "I have been told to wait for you, and I am tired. It is good that you are here."

I felt so near to him that I soon confessed my sins—I had never done as much for another. I would have deemed it belittling to whatever pride I had as a man. (For my sins were too small.) I might be a master carpenter and thirty years of age, but I felt young before him, and modest and much too innocent for such a grave man. I searched to find evil in myself and came back with no more than moments I could recall of disrespect toward my mother and contests in the night with lustful thoughts. Perhaps there had been a few acts of unkindness when judging others.

"Well," he said, "you can still repent. Our sin is always more than we know." And John came behind me as I entered the water, and with the strength of a desert lion, he seized me by the nose and, with his other hand pressing upon my forehead, thrust me back into the river. Passing so quickly from air to water, I gasped first at my loss of breath and then from all the water I swallowed. Still, in this moment I saw many things, and my life was changed forever.

Was the Holiest descending toward us in the shape of a dove? And when I came up from the water, the dove was on my shoulder. I felt as if much had come back to me from all that had been lost. I was one again with myself— a poor man, but good. And then I felt more. I had a vision of glory. The heavens opened for an instant and it was as if I saw a million souls.

I heard a voice, and it came from the heavens. It came into my ear and said: "Before I formed thee in the belly, I knew thee." Fear and exaltation were in me then, and in greater measure than I had ever known. I raised my face to the heavens and said, "Lord God, I am like a child."

And the Lord spoke as He had to the prophet Jeremiah. I heard: "Say not 'I am a child,' for you shall go to all the places that I shall send thee." And I felt as if His finger blessed my mouth even as the beak of the dove touched my lips. His Word came into me like the burning fire in my bones when I was twelve and sick with fever.

Now John withdrew his hand from my head and we stood in the river. Away went the dove. And John and I spoke to each other a little. I will tell of that, and soon. But when I left, I knew that I would never see him again. He began to sing as I left, but it was to the River Jordan, not to me. And the taste of that brown river was still in my mouth and the dust of the desert in my nostrils as I set out on my long march home to Nazareth.

11

It was late in the afternoon. The light upon the rocks turned to gold. And I could still hear John the Baptist as he sang. Since he knew no song, the music of his throat came forth like the voice of a ram.

I walked with strength. For now I was no longer like other men. My legs took larger strides than before. Now I knew the other man who had lived within the shell of myself, and he was better than me. I had become that man.

A great cloud came over the sky. There was a downpour. A rainbow arose from one end of the desert to touch the other, and above me was the radiance of the Lord. Soon I lay down upon the hot damp sand, and soon I heard His voice. He said: "Stand upon your feet."

When I did, He told me: "Once I spoke to the prophet Ezekiel and he saved our people in Babylon. Now these words given to Ezekiel are for you: 'Son of Man, I send thee to the children of Israel, to a nation that hath rebelled against Me, even unto this very day. For they are impudent children and stiff-hearted. But you will speak My words unto them. Since they are not a people of a strange speech whose words you cannot understand but are the house of Israel, behold! I will make your face strong against their face. So fear them not.'"

Then this voice said into my ear: "Those were My words to Ezekiel. But to you I say: You are My son, and therefore you will be mightier than a prophet. Even mightier than the prophet Ezekiel."

I still had many hours to travel across land I hardly knew. Again I was full of exaltation, and again I was full of fear. I was also weary. The scrolls I had studied since childhood were not as close to me as the words of this high Lord my God, yet now that He was near, I could only fear Him. For the sound of His voice can be heard in the echo of great rocks when they fall. And I did not know how to serve a Lord who could leave boils upon the flesh of every man and beast in the land of Egypt and cast hail to blight every herb of the field, or fire in the grass until every tree was consumed. I raised my hands toward heaven as if to ask whether I was truly the one to exercise His force. And God said to me, "Since you are not yet strong, do not return to your home. Go up rather into the mountain that is there before you. Go now. In that wilderness, fast among the rocks. Drink the water that is beneath the rocks. But eat no food. Before the sun sets on the last of your days of fast, you will know why I have chosen you."

Soon I learned of His power to protect me. As I climbed, darkness fell and I had to share my ground with serpents and scorpions. Yet none came near. In the morning I climbed further and for much of the day upward on this mountain. And it was worthy of the lamentations of the prophet Isaiah, for one could say that the cormorant and the bittern possessed it.

In every direction was emptiness. On the ramparts of the rock, vultures looked down on me, side by side, every vulture with her mate. It was then I thought of how John the Baptist had asked, on saying farewell: "Did the light of the Lord appear when you were immersed?"

Even as John's eyes stared into mine, I had wondered if the million million of souls that I had seen were the face of the Lord. But to John I said only: "Is it not death and destruction to see Him?"

He replied: "For all but the Christ." Then John said: "Once the Holy Spirit came to me. He was so near that I put my hands before my eyes. But the Holy Spirit said: 'I will let you gaze upon My back,' and He allowed me to see that His back was noble, a noble back." Then John grasped my arm. "I have known since I was a child that my cousin must come after me and replace me. For my mother spoke of how your mother told her of all that had been with her." Now he kissed me on both cheeks. "I baptize with water," he said, "and can cleanse any soul who has truly repented, even as water can extinguish fire. But you will baptize with the Spirit. You will root out evil with God's mercy." And he kissed me again.

It was hard not to remember the breath of John the Baptist when he embraced me, for it was full of all that is in the odor of an exhausted man. And indeed, no matter how often one seeks water to soothe the throat, such an odor cannot be separated from the flesh. A vast fatigue speaks of all that has been lost to one's striving. Yet his skin had been honest and full of the loneliness of the desert and its rocks. And so did he also smell of the waters of the River Jordan and the heavy wisdom of its mud and silt.

12

At the summit, the rocks stood about like tombs, and the steps between were treacherous. It was midday. The heat of the sun was on me.

I sat in the shadow of a great stone and looked out on the lands of Israel, upon Galilee to the north and Judea to the south. The haze had a golden hue, and I wondered whether one could even see the spires of gold that rose above the hills of the holy city. But I did not think long on Jerusalem; living without food for a day, I was hungry.

Yet I also knew why the Lord had sent me to the summit of this mountain. For it was not enough to be His son and cousin to John the Baptist. I had to pass through trials, and the first test must be not to eat. Even as I said to myself, "I will take no food until sundown," the Lord replied.

I did not see Him, nor did I feel His presence other than His voice (which was in my ear), but He said: "You will fast until I tell you to eat."

So I was without food for that day and the next. And by the fifth day, when the pangs of my stomach had given way to a solemn emptiness of spirit, I felt weak and no longer knew if I had the strength to climb down from this mountain. So I said aloud, "How long, O Lord?" and He replied, "Long. It will be long."

Since I was not there to dispute Him but to follow His will, fasting grew easier. I shielded myself from the sun and came to love the taste of water and the wisdom that is found in the shade of large rocks (until they grow too cold at night for any wisdom). And the air of night was cold. No plants grew on the summit of this mountain. Which was just as well. For there were hours when I could have chewed on their thorns.

In the second week, I had visions of King David and knew that he had committed a great sin. I could not recall the offense, but I did remember that he had been punished, and on his death the Lord had appeared to the son of David, King Solomon, and asked: "What shall I give thee?"

And Solomon replied: "O Lord my God, I know not how

to go out nor to come in, and Thy servant is in the midst of Thy people, a great people that cannot be numbered nor counted. Give therefore Thy servant an understanding heart that I may discern between good and bad."

And I recalled how this speech had so pleased the Lord that He said to Solomon: "Because thou hast not asked for a long life nor for riches nor begged for the death of thine enemies but asked for discernment in judgment, then, behold, I have given thee a wise and understanding heart."

And God gave Solomon all that he had not asked for, both riches and honors, until there were no kings as great as Solomon in those days.

But now the voice of the Lord was saying to me: "Solomon did not keep My Commandments. Solomon spoke three thousand proverbs, and his songs were a thousand and five. All people came to hear the wisdom of Solomon, in that he exceeded all the kings of the earth. And these kings brought him silver, ivory, apes, and peacocks. But," said the Lord to my ear, "King Solomon loved many strange women: the daughter of Pharaoh and the women of the Moabites, the Ammonites, the Edomites, the Sedonians, and the Hittites, whereas I had said unto the children of Israel, 'Ye shall not go in to them. For surely they will turn your heart toward their gods.' But Solomon had seven hundred wives and three hundred concubines, and when Solomon was old, his heart was not perfect with Me. I had given him too many gifts. So," said the Lord, "I will not give you riches. And you will never tarry with a woman, or you shall lose the Lord."

He had given me Solomon's sins on which to meditate, and that was an advantage not given to Solomon. I, being without food, had no desire for a woman, nor did I feel at odds with the Lord's decision. My fast continued.

The prophets were often with me in these weeks: Elijah and Elisha, Isaiah and Daniel and Ezekiel. I could recall their words as if they were my own. Before long, I had a dream that made me one with the prophet Elijah, and in this dream I had contests with the prophets of Baal. More than forty such pagan prophets had come to my mountain to sacrifice a bullock, but first they destroyed the Lord's altar on the summit. Then they lacerated themselves with knives to show their devotion to Baal. Blood spurted from the wounds of these prophets and they cried aloud, yet the god Baal could not speak.

Seeing that Baal was silent in my presence, I put twelve large stones on end, to stand for the twelve tribes of the sons of Israel, after which I restored the altar of the Lord. Then I dug a trench around the stones and put wood on the altar and cut the bullock into pieces, laying the raw flesh upon the wood. And then I poured four barrels of water on the sacrifice until this water ran into the trench.

And the fire of the Lord blazed through the meat of the bullock and the sopping wood and the wet stones and licked up all the water that was in the trench. And I be-

headed these forty prophets of Baal with a sword, and
only then did I awake.

Now it came to me that I was not Elijah but only dream-
ing of the scroll of Elijah, and the dream had been there
to tell me that my fast must continue for forty days and
forty nights. For if I did not change my ways or the people of Israel did not change theirs, then all of us were in
danger of God's final judgment.

So could I also see how my youth had passed with more
thought given to the wood under my tools than to my people. Nor had I listened when Joseph would say: "All share
in the sinfulness of Israel because we do not work hard
enough to overcome it."

I was yet to learn that I would care about sinners more
than for the pious, but now I was content to quote the
words of Isaiah to myself: "Though Thy people Israel be
as the sand of the sea, yet a remnant shall return." And
there, near to the sixth week of my fast, full of the spirit of
Isaiah, I hoped that with the aid of this remnant of good
Jews I might recover all that had been lost in the nation.
So I would repeat the sayings of Isaiah aloud, speaking
even into the eye of the sun until my eyes burned and I
was obliged to return to the shade. I pondered the prayers
I would use with sinners and decided that I would tell
them, even as had Isaiah: " 'Wash you, make you clean;
put away the evil of your doings; relieve the oppressed.' "

And it was the fortieth day. As evening came, the Lord

said to me, "Tomorrow you may step down from the mountain and take food." Hunger came back to me on these words, and I was ravenous.

Yet even as I was thinking of what I would eat, the Lord said, "Tonight, remain on the mountain. A visitor will come."

13

The visitor soon arrived. And he was as handsome as a prince. He had a gold ornament on a gold chain about his neck, and in this ornament was the face of a ram, bestial yet more noble than any ram I had ever seen. And the hair of this prince was as long as my own and lustrous. He was dressed in robes of velvet that were as purple as the late evening, and he wore a crown as golden as the sun. He had climbed the mountain, yet there was no dust on his robes nor sweat upon his skin. He could be no other than who I thought, and indeed he soon introduced himself. I said to myself, "The Devil is the most beautiful creature God ever made."

His first words were: "Do you know how the prophet Isaiah met his death?"

I was overcome with silence. So I was obliged to listen as he said: "Isaiah was killed by a Jewish king, the pagan Manasseh, cohort of Amon. A bad Jew." The Devil nodded as if he were a good Jew (which I was certain he was not!). Then he held up one finger and spoke again: "This Manasseh, wishing to destroy the religion of his fathers, sent out a royal order that Isaiah was to be uprooted from his home in the city and hunted like an animal. Hearing of this, Isaiah fled, and the soldiers of Manasseh set out after him into the wilderness. There, the prophet looked for a tree with a hollow large enough for a man to stand inside. This sanctuary," said the Devil, "he found in a stout oak with a rotten center, and he placed himself inside it. But the officers of Manasseh discovered where he was hiding and brought a great saw to the tree and cut it in half. Isaiah went screaming into his death. Did you know?" asked the Devil.

"I did not hear of such a death."

Whereupon he laughed. I felt weakened by this story more than by any deprivation of the fast.

He, however, was not about to cease speaking. "The manner in which Isaiah met his death need not give you large concern," he said, "since you are not a prophet but indeed the Son! To my recollection, which is not small, the Lord has never performed an act of this kind before.

46

Indeed, to look upon you is to give me much to contemplate. For you seem innocent of all that I know."

He looked at me fondly. His eyes were black marble, but there were lights within. He said, "Are you hungry? Are you in need of drink?" And he brought forth a jug of wine and a leg of lamb, well cooked, which I had not seen beneath his robes until he produced them. And now he approached me so closely that my nostrils took in the spirit of the wine and the gravies of the lamb, even the smell of the Devil himself, which penetrated a small cloud of perfume rising from the folds of his robe. I could also perceive how greed came forth from his body. For that was kin to the odor that lives between the buttocks. Therefore I refused his food, but still, the other odors of his body entered my appetite like the savor that comes from an oven when food is roasting. And he, seeing such deliberation, smiled once more and said, "But of course you have no need of food. Being the Son of God, you can as easily command these stones to be bread. Which is proper food for an Essene. However, your garment is neither clean nor free of dust. Indeed, that you are the Son of God surprises me. Why did your Father choose you? Say to Him when next you converse that I salute Him. For do you know? Your Father and I have had much traffic and considerable dispute, and so We are always eager to obtain word of the Other and His doings. Indeed, on those occasions when We meet, I tell Him that men and women are the crown

47

of all He has conceived among the animals and the plants of the field but that it is I, not He, who has a better understanding of this Creation. For His work has given issue to many small creatures and spirits that He hardly knows as well as I do. Of course, I was once His servant, His most trusted servant. Contemplate, then, how well I understand Him."

I was amazed. He did not inspire fear but comfort. Now I knew how it might feel to be a sinner in a low tavern drinking wine. The labors of this long fast were gone; I felt balm come to my limbs. I could talk to the Devil; he was comfortable. If his odor could leave me uneasy, it also offered sympathy to desires I had not yet allowed myself to feel.

Yet if I would allow him much, still I could not agree that God, the Lord of the Universe, did not understand His Creation better than my visitor. "It is not possible," I exclaimed. "He is all-powerful. The heavens and the earth, the stars and the sun, bow before Him. They do not bow to you."

For one moment, Satan snorted like a horse. Was he unwilling to accept the bridle?

"Your Father," said the Devil, "is but one god among many. You might take account of the myriad respected by the Romans. Are we to give no homage to the great will of the Romans? Why, your Father does not even have the power to command His own Jews in their own land even though so many see Him as the only One. You would do better to consider the breadth of His rages; they are unseemly for a great god. They are swollen and without proportion. He issues too many threats. He cannot bear anyone who would dispute Him. Whereas I confide to you that a hint of disobedience and a whiff of treachery are among the joys of life, and are to be ranked with its spoils rather than its evils."

"That is not so," I was able to answer. "My Father is God, and of many dimensions, and of all dimensions." But my words tasted like straw.

The Devil replied, "He is not in command of Himself!"

14

Nor did the Devil show any fear at what he had said. He continued to speak. "Your Father," he said, "does not have the right to demand complete obedience from His people. He does not comprehend that women are creatures different from men and live with separate understanding. Indeed, your Father has no inkling of women; His scorn for them is shared by His prophets, who speak, so they claim, with His voice. And they do! For rarely will He reprimand them! Look at Isaiah! Tell me that Isaiah does not live in your Father's heart when he says: 'Because the daughters of Zion are haughty and walk with stretched-forth necks and wanton eyes, walking and mincing as they go, therefore the Lord will smite with a scabbard the crown of the head of the daughters of Zion, and the Lord will discover their secret parts.' *Their secret parts*," repeated the Devil. And he continued to speak with the words of Isaiah: " 'The Lord will take away their bracelets and bonnets, the ornaments of the legs, the earrings, the rings and the nose-jewels, the fine linen, the hoods and the veils. And it shall come to pass that instead of sweet smell there shall be stink; and instead of a girdle, a rent; for lovely hair, there shall be baldness, and burning instead of beauty.' "

"My Father was speaking of the nation of Zion," I said. "So were we taught."

"No," replied the Devil. "He pretends to speak of the nation of Zion. But it is women He belittles. His mighty curses He saves for the men. When He wishes to address the nation of Israel, He is speaking only to men: 'The indignation of the Lord is upon all nations, and His fury upon all their armies: He hath utterly destroyed them, He hath delivered them to the slaughter. Their offal shall come up out of their carcasses and the mountains shall be melted with their blood.' What a rage! His failures burn in His heart! Can He suspect that He may not be all-powerful? No! He does not have enough spirit to say: 'Yes, I have lost, but my soldiers were honest and fought well.' No, He is vengeful. 'The palaces will be forsaken,' says Isaiah, 'the forts and towers shall be dens forever, until the Spirit be poured upon us from on High.'

"But when," asked the Devil, "will the Spirit be poured

upon us? Your Father would send you forth to improve the hearts of men when His own heart is caked with the blood of those He has slaughtered. His love of all He has created is choked by His curses. His rages may be mighty, but they do not satisfy His desire. His language reveals how much He adores the grandeur He pretends to despise.

"Tell me that your Father is not filled with an adoration of women. Which He hides from Himself! For He hates their power to entice Him. Ezekiel knows what is in your Father's heart. After all, he heard these words from the Lord: 'I swore unto thee and entered into a covenant with thee, and thou becamest mine. I washed thee with water; yea, I thoroughly washed away thy blood, and I anointed thee with oil. I clothed thee also in broidered work, and fine linen, and I covered thee with silk, with ornaments, and I put bracelets upon thy hands and a chain on thy neck, and earrings in thine ears, and a beautiful crown upon thine head. Thou wast decked with gold and silver; thou didst eat fine bread, and honey, and oil: and thou wast exceedingly beautiful, and thou didst prosper into a kingdom. And thy renown went forth among the heathen for thy beauty which I had put upon thee.' Now," said the Devil, "hear how He complains! He is pitiful in His complaints: 'But thou didst trust in thine own beauty, and played the harlot because of thy renown, and poured out thy fornications on everyone that passed by, and multiplied thy whoredoms. Thou hast also committed fornication with the Egyptians, thy neighbors, great of flesh; and hast played the whore also with the Assyrians because thou wast insatiable.

"'Wherefore, O harlot, because thy filthiness was poured out, and thy nakedness discovered, therefore I will gather all thy lovers with whom thou hast taken pleasure; and will gather them round about against thee, and give thee into their hand, and they shall throw down thine eminent place, and shall strip thee of thy clothes, and shall take thy fair jewels and leave thee naked and bare, and they shall stone thee, and thrust thee through with their swords. And they shall burn thy houses with fire, and execute judgments upon thee in the sight of many women: and I will cause thee to cease from playing the harlot.'

"Does all this take place," asked the Devil, "in order to scorn Jerusalem? Say rather that your Father's language reeks of desire."

"Your words are pollutions." I hoped to excite enough anger in myself to reply, but I could only repeat: "Your words are poisonous."

Satan replied: "Your Father's tongue is as ripe with lust as my own."

I knew confusion. Could I deny that my loins had quickened as I listened to the repetition of my Father's words?

Now the Devil said: "You believe that you are sitting on the summit of this mountain, but we are no longer there. We have risen to a place above the holy places."

His embrace of my vision was complete. Now I saw the city of Jerusalem, and it was beneath us. For we were no longer seated on the mountain. We were on the highest dome of the Great Temple in Jerusalem.

I felt vertigo.

At that moment the Devil said to me, "Because you are the Son of God, you can feel free to leap! Cast yourself out. Your Father's angels will carry you."

I felt a temptation to jump. But, most suddenly, I did not feel as if I were the Son of God. Not yet!

An abyss was below me. And I knew it would be there for all the generations to come. Whenever they stood on a height, they would live in the wind of that unruly spirit who dwells in our breath and has a terror of the leap. Now the Devil looked at me again with his dark eyes, and the points of light within were like a night of stars; those eyes would promise glory. "If you stay with your Father you will labor for Him," he said. "You will be consumed. Jump! You can save yourself. Jump!"

I would be smashed. But would my extinction be brief? And my return to the living as quick? The Devil had taken me into him. By the light in his dark eyes, I knew his speech even though he said nothing. If I jumped, the Devil would possess me. I would have leaped to my death at his bidding.

But at this moment he said aloud, "You will be reborn. In secret: God will not know. I have the power to distract."

He was telling me of a life to come. It would be bountiful. "All is mine!" cried Satan aloud.

Indeed, greed was godly to him. Out of crude greed would come works of great power. "Those who have loyalty to me," said the Devil, "sit now upon the earth with such command that they never give vent to those little turds, fit only for a goat, that pinch themselves forth from the bony cheeks of your friend John. Why, he will not even relieve himself on the Sabbath! And on other days he carries a small hoe to cover his leavings."

And I, in this same moment, wondered whether I could leap but not fall. Could I fly with angels? By power given to me by the Lord, could I fly?

Could I know? Satan stood between my Father and me. Did he have the power to deny the wings of the angel? I did not jump. I wanted to, but I did not dare. To myself I said, "I will not serve God as a brave son but as a modest one." That was just. Had I not spent more than half my life working carefully with many small movements, equal to equal, with the small mysteries of wood?

And now I had an inkling of why God had chosen Mary and Joseph to be my family. I said, "Get thee hence, Satan." If my voice was weak, I repeated it: "Get thee hence, Satan," and now my voice had more force. It was ready to draw upon the strength that comes from emptiness. And I saw the wisdom of the Lord. For even in fasting is strength, and that was the greatest strength one could bring to bear against the Devil inasmuch as he hated emptiness. Who is more lonely than the Devil? I had the power at last to look into Satan's eyes and say: "It is not you I want. It is my Father." Even as I said this, I knew a small but sharp woe. I was losing something I desired, and I was losing it forever.

But Satan gave a cry like a beast just wounded by the spear. "Your Father," he cried, "will destroy His own Creation. For too little!" And he departed. And I was left with a vision of angels. They gathered about me to bathe my eyes. I slept. Never before had I known such exhaustion.

In the morning I awoke to see myself on this same mountain where I had lived for forty days. Now I was ready to come down. The road to Nazareth would be long and empty. Yet for the next day and the next, no brigands attacked. And that was fortunate for me. My hour with the Devil had left me spent. My breath was foul. Nor did I feel that I had escaped altogether.

I was, however, not distraught. For as I marched, so could I recite the words of Isaiah: " 'Unto us,' " I declared, " 'a child is born; unto us a son is given; and the government shall be upon his shoulders; and his name shall be called wonderful, counselor, the mighty God, the everlasting Father, the prince of peace.' " And if I was too insignificant for such words, I had to suppose that God had chosen me for His son because I had been born and had lived in the midst of common people rather than like a king. Thereby I could understand many small virtues and weak habits in others. If I could increase in my powers (and I knew that He would pass on many powers to me), perhaps the world of men might multiply in virtue with me. So I had begun to believe in my Father. I would labor for Him. Soon He would come to save Jerusalem. He was Lord of the Universe. I would labor with joy. Through Him, comfort would come to those who were sorrowful, and the hungry would be fed, yes, and those sinners in greatest despair would find their sins remitted. And I felt such joy at these thoughts that I could not believe they were my own. Indeed, the Devil must have scraped me sore in my judgment, for I was now ready to do all. But then, on this new morning I was not much afraid of Satan. He had captured only a small part of me. I had been tested, had proved loyal, and now my tongue began to feel clean. As I walked, there was the smallest and sweetest of modest miracles. In this desert waste I came upon a small tree and it bore plums that slaked my thirst and gave a sweet warmth to my limbs. I fell to my knees and blessed my Creator, yet before I could even begin to pray, I came to my feet again.

I was obliged to wonder. Why had the Lord left me alone with Satan? Was it to scourge me of an excess of piety? Before long I would learn that there might be truth in this. There was work to do, and it could not be accomplished on one's knees.

15

I returned to Nazareth and entered the house where I lived with my mother. On greeting me, she was much relieved. For more than forty days I had been away, and if she had supposed at first that I was on a journey with my cousin, she had soon begun to hear fearful stories concerning John. (And all of this had come to pass while I was on the mountain.) It seemed that Herod Antipas, the son of dead King Herod, had long distrusted John the Baptist. Like his father, Antipas suffered from dreams; he worried that the prophet would inspire people to rise against him. Whereupon he put John away in a dungeon in the fortress of Machaerus on the high cliffs over the

Dead Sea. So I knew that my time had come. I must leave Nazareth. I must take up a life of preaching and try to emulate what John had done.

Yet my mother thought I should not be a preacher. She did not care to think of me wandering on lonely roads to give blessings to strangers; better, by far, to become a good Essene. She wanted me to join the desert community at Qumran, where the most devout are gathered. But that was not my desire. Men who choose to live at Qumran must first confess all guilt and all sin, give all that they own to the brethren, and live among them for years before they can be accepted as true Essenes of Qumran. And one did not speak in the presence of one's leaders unless invited.

I did not understand how my mother could want such a life for me. It was the Lord to whom I should submit myself for tests, not to this or that High Priest. But then, my mother was not always easy to understand. If she was proud of my origin, she was full of worry for my well-being; rare was the day when she did not expect a catastrophe to befall me. Fear lived like a night animal in our small house. One could all but hear the scurrying in the dark.

Moreover, if Mary was modest, she was also vain, and I would suffer by both ends, for her will was graven in stone. Yet she did not see herself as strong, but frail. Worse! She saw me as being like her, and therefore unready to go out into the world. And I, knowing all that I must now attempt, was not pleased that she placed such small confidence in me.

I did not tell her what had happened during my forty days on the mountain, but then she must have known that I had been near at last to my Father. Still, she did not wish to hear any part of that. She had a heart large enough for a queen, but like a queen, she did not enjoy what she could not understand.

Yet she was also a mother. She knew me very well. So she could now surmise that it had not only been my Father who was with me on the mountain but the Other. If the Devil owned the powers of darkness, then I was weak enough, as she would see it, to have been tainted. Therefore I must be guided by a community of the most devout. It can be said: She did not make my way easier. I was unhappy with her forebodings; she had the power to foretell certain events.

In the midst of this quiet but unyielding dispute there came a diversion. A marriage was taking place in Cana, a town not far from Nazareth. The father of the bride, a wealthy man who had once hired Joseph and his carpenters to construct a fine house, now invited my mother, myself, and my brothers, James and John, to this wedding. And it would be the first time that Mary had left her home since Joseph died. Indeed, she remained so doubtful of whether to go or not to go that by the time we arrived, it was late and the ceremony had ended. My mother, most embarrassed, looked about sharply and said, "They are without wine." So many had come from the village to celebrate that all the wine was gone.

Her voice was telling me that when a nuptial feast becomes dry, happiness will soon depart; it is an omen of misery for the new husband and wife. So I thought to try such powers as might now belong to me.

Before us were six large stone jars of water, and on a table was one red grape, no more, and that grape I ate slowly and with much contemplation of the Spirit who resided within. Indeed, I could feel an angel at my side. In that instant, the water in the jars became wine. I knew this. It had been accomplished by no more than the clear taste of one grape and the presence of one angel.

I felt near to the Kingdom of God. For now I knew that this Kingdom was composed of much beauty. My Father was not only the God of wrath but could offer tenderness as gentle as the concern that rests in the touch of one's hand. All the same, I was also full of sorrow. For I had a vision of a great feast that I would never see. Before long, therefore, I chose to leave; James and John could walk home with my mother.

As I left I could hear the uncle of the bride speak to the groom: "Every host sets forth good wine at the beginning, but when all are drunk, then wine which is not as good is presented. Yet you kept your best wine for the end and so your marriage will be blessed."

That was the first of my miracles, and took place in

Cana of Galilee. I was not quick, however, to praise myself, since the angel sent by my Father whispered into my thoughts: "Even as a barrel overflowing with honey can soon be emptied, so does the foolish son scatter his store of miracles." Therefore, I did not tell my mother. She was merely pleased that there had been wine after all, and so she was of slightly better heart concerning my departure. In the morning I set out with no more than a staff, a cloak, my sandals, and her tears.

16

I had thought of preaching in Capernaum, half a day's walk from Nazareth. Despite what the Devil had told me, I still wished to think of the prophet Isaiah as my guide, and he had written: "By way of the sea beyond Jordan, in Galilee of the gentiles, the people who sat in darkness saw a great light." So I chose Capernaum. It was on the Sea of Galilee (which is only a lake but as large as a sea), and the River Jordan flowed south from there to Jerusalem.

Before leaving for Capernaum, however, I decided to speak at the synagogue in Nazareth. Since my tongue was hardly the equal of my hands when they worked with wood, I thought to begin where some, at least, would know me.

But at first I could say no more to the congregation than: "Repent, for the Kingdom of Heaven is at hand. The end is near." These words brought back no more than silence. How could people wish the Day of Judgment to be on them, and so soon? Indeed, it was a sunny morning in Nazareth. I, full of new thoughts that faith, even when severe, must still be natural, as natural as breath, also said (and now I spoke in our ancient Hebrew): "I thank Thee, O Father, because Thou hast hid these things from the wise and prudent and hast revealed them unto babes."

Later I would see what Luke wrote in his gospel.

"And all they in the synagogue when they heard these things," wrote Luke, "were filled with wrath. And rose up and thrust him out of the city, and led him onto the brow of a hill whereon their city was built that they might cast him down headlong. But he, passing through the midst of them, went his way."

Luke was not a Jew. So his account is rank with exaggeration; he hated Jews. Because I was speaking in the small synagogue to which I had gone from childhood, none were ready to scoff at me. Still, I could feel laughter creep out of their feet. Such derision was like mice scampering silently over my toes. Indeed, I could hear the whispers before they were spoken: "The carpenter tells us to repent." And others said, "What is this that the Lord hides from the wise and prudent but offers unto babes?"

So I knew that I must learn to preach in places where I was not known. That much I vowed, and yet, as I took the road from Nazareth to Capernaum, I could feel how my heart was still bruised by what the Devil had dared to say against the Lord. And my Father had not even defended Himself.

At that instant, in the midst of such thoughts, I stumbled on the road, and it was an odd misstep. I was lithe of foot, yet I fell heavily. A strong arm had hurled me to the earth. And a strong voice spoke into my ear: "The words of the prophets are not My words. My prophets are honest but full of excess."

I only said: "My Lord, I feel weak. I am lacking in eloquence."

"Yes," the Lord said, "so did Moses say: 'O Lord, I am slow of speech and with a slow tongue.' I told him as I tell you: 'Who made man's mouth? Am I not the Lord?' Therefore, go, and I will be with your mouth and I will teach you what to say. Your words will not fall on the ground."

Given this promise, I felt less uncertain. My Father also said, "You can do well in Capernaum. Say but one thing many times. These people are like stones and they are deaf. Therefore, tell them again and again: 'Thus saith the Lord God.' Do not be concerned with whether they hear. Words are also My creatures, and they travel by many roads."

As I came to my feet, I could feel the Spirit lifting me higher. And I heard the wings of invisible creatures flying about me, then the sound of a thousand chariots, a noise of happy clamor that might as well have come from the other side of a hill. The Lord spoke again: "When you believe in Me, miracles will be in your hands, your eyes, and your voice."

Yes, the hand of the Lord was strong. I came to Capernaum.

17

As I walked beside the pebbled shore of the Sea of Galilee, I saw two fishermen casting their nets. They were powerful men, and large, and with large hands. The older, who looked younger than myself, was, I would soon learn, named Simon; the other was his brother, Andrew. I also saw how Simon, once he had drawn in many fish, came upon a tear in his net and with strips of rawhide he mended this flaw with dexterity.

I thought to myself, There is need of a man who can mend nets. If by one skill he captures the fish, by another does he prevent losing them. And without caution, as my voice carried across the distance it would take to cast a small stone, I said, "Come with me and I will make you fishers of men." I said it with great merriment, for I realized that to be without one's fellows for forty days is also a fast. If I had seen men and women at the wedding and in the synagogue of Nazareth, still they were not of my choice, not friends or men with whom I might work.

So I looked upon these two fishermen as good men, and liked how they cast their nets to put a small spell upon the sea. Being a carpenter, who knew less of water than of wood, it still seemed to me that fish would be protected by their own spell and so a fisherman would need his own power of spirit to draw such creatures into his net.

And so, "Yes," I said, and was rich in my enthusiasm. "Come with me and I will make you fishers of men." Between their eyes and mine passed an agreement across this space of water; I could feel how God had enabled me to steal a few skills from the Devil.

In truth, I could now employ Satan's manner when speaking. I would address strangers with the finest courtesy and the most intimate exhilaration, as if we shared among ourselves the wonder of many things unsaid.

I recalled how as Satan departed he had said to me, "Having high regard for you, I would like to touch your hand." And because I had wanted him to leave, I had touched my right hand to his, and knew in the same instant that I had surrendered a share of the Lord's protection.

Only a small share. And I was certain that God had

taken much back from Satan. For no sooner had Simon and Andrew brought their boat to shore and filled their bags with their catch than they came with me down the road to a house, where I was introduced to James, the son of Zebedee, and John, his brother, and this I saw as a good omen (those being the same names as my two brothers). I know that as soon as Simon called to them, they left their father, Zebedee, alone with his hired servants and came along with us, and I had to wonder if they were more ready for diversion than for prayer. Yet Simon vouched for them, and Simon would be my rock. So I decided. Soon I began to call him Simon Peter, for Peter, while it is the Greek name for rock, is a good sound. And Peter would be my rock in all hours but one.

To Capernaum I now marched with these four followers. Looking at them, I knew that I had more to honor than to distrust. As we walked, Peter drew me aside and said: "Two nights ago our nets were so heavy with fish that our boat was foundering. But I prayed and we were saved. I would tell you: In my prayer I saw your face."

Peter now fell on his knees and declared: "Do not take me with you, for I am a sinful man, O Lord." But I grasped his hand and told him that he was a good man as well as I could measure it. And I also said that his presence would strengthen me in Capernaum. So there we went, and straightaway to the synagogue. And on this morning I preached the wisdom of John the Baptist.

It was the Sabbath, and many were there. I understood that if I had found Peter and Andrew and James and John at their labors on the Sabbath, it was because they did not keep a mark of the days on which work was forbidden. Fishermen know only when the waters are ready. So I also knew that they would not be learned enough to preach with me. Not on this day. Yet I was eloquent after all, and by myself.

I spoke of God's heart and how it was heavy. Out of the multitude of men and women that the Lord had created, He had selected His own chosen people, His Jews. Now, in these days, some were faithful, but many were not. God had prepared a heaven, therefore, to take in those Jews that He could judge with happiness.

Those, however, who betrayed the Law or chased after sin or were full of folly would suffer. It would be a judgment to descend through many depths, cell beneath cell, even as the stone steps of my Father's dungeon go down forever, step by step. So do sinners recognize, and too late, that the power of His hand can destroy a kingdom as easily as a mouse is trodden underfoot! I spoke with the force of a man who swings a sword.

"Repent," I said, "and you will have remission of all your sins." And by repeating this doctrine of John the Baptist, I could speak with authority. My voice lifted above the singsong of Pharisees and scribes. In this synagogue of Capernaum, as in others, the Pharisees and

70

scribes would read from the scrolls in a weak and whin-ing song, a droning of the heart as if their throats, dulled by years of compromise, spoke only from dying coals. Their voices hissed forth. Whereas my voice was full.

I said—nor did I know I would say as much until my words rang forth—"Come unto me, all who labor and are heavy laden, and I will give you rest. Take my yoke upon you and learn from me; for I am meek and lowly in heart and you will find rest for your souls. Yet I would also say" —and saying this, felt as if new powers had again been granted to me—"if you ask, 'Lord, will you cast out dev-ils?' then they will be cast out."

It was as I said. It was exactly as I said. A man came for-ward from the congregation, and I could see that he frightened others, for he looked like a brigand. His nose was broken, and many scars were on his face—an old brute with a spirit so unclean that the stench of his body came before him. Yet he cried out, "What have we to do with you, Yeshua of Nazareth? Are you come to destroy us?"

And I saw that his features were thickened by the blows he had received in payment for the unrest within him. So I stood in my place as he approached. I stared into his eyes and said, "Hold your peace." And he did not move.

I knew that a foul presence had to be drawn forth from his heart even as a small beast is torn from a burrow, and I knew that he had come to me so that this demon could be expelled. Nor did I need a magician's ring or aromatic herbs to place beneath his nostrils. With one breath, I said no more than: "Demon, come forth. Come out!"

And an evil being tore out of his throat. It cried aloud in a bestial voice.

This unclean spirit was invisible. Yet all could see that the presence had been cast forth into the midst of the synagogue. Empty benches fell over, and there was a wind on the floor, and dust. Then all such disturbance was gone.

The good Jews of the synagogue were amazed. They were pious people, and their greatest uneasiness was to share a room with these unclean spirits. They did not know how to resist them. Therefore they desired no traffic with people who were ready to war with evil. They now said: "What new doctrine is this? Who does he command? Is it unclean?"

In that moment I felt as if I had hurled a stone into the midst of the Sea of Galilee and ripples had traveled to every shore. Word of my deed would pass through all the regions about us.

"Ask," I said to them who were in the synagogue.

"Ask, and it shall be given unto you.

"Seek, and you shall find.

"Knock, and it shall be opened to you."

My new friends Simon Peter and Andrew and James and John came out of the synagogue and went back with me to the house of Simon Peter.

18

So alive was I with new strength that when we came into Peter's house and his wife's mother was lying there with a fever, I had only to take her by the hand and the fever left. She rose from her bed and was delighted and cooked for us. We were well fed.

In the evening, friends of Simon and Andrew and James and John came to the house with men and women who thought they were possessed of devils. I felt full of wonder and happiness at my new skill and cures came quickly. I had no more than to put my hand upon someone, and out came many small devils.

Then, in the morning, Peter said to me, "People seek for

you now, and I fear they will be many. I would warn you. They are curious. They wish to witness miracles. But will that give you the power to change men's souls?"

His speech made me think of John the Baptist in the dungeon of Herod Antipas. Pain came like a knife to slash at my chest. For if the Lord gave me great talents, then I would be open to vengeance from those who hated the Lord. So I encouraged Peter and Andrew and James and John to leave with me. We would move on to other synagogues in Galilee and cast out devils there. It would be better to do the deed and leave each throng with wonder than to remain in one circle until such wonder became our noose. And I knew that now I was thinking with the wisdom of Peter.

In the courtyard of another synagogue in another town, a leper came to me and asked, "Can you make me clean?" When I was silent, he said, "Until I am clean, I cannot enter the synagogue. Yet if I cannot enter, how can I become clean?"

I did not know how to cure a leper. Yet I could not turn away from his eyes. So I whispered to the Lord, "Grant me this power on this day."

Looking at the man, and being careful not to avert my eyes in horror, I was able to remember that it was written in the scrolls that God had said to Moses: "Cast your rod on the ground." And when he did, the rod became a serpent. So soon as it moved, Moses fled. But the Lord told him: "Do not run. Put forth thy hand and take it by the tail."

Moses caught the serpent, and it became again a rod in his hand. The Lord said: "Put down thy hand unto thy bosom," and Moses did as he was told, but when he took his hand out, his fingers were as leprous as snow. Then God said, "Put back thy hand in thy bosom," and Moses did, and this time when he withdrew it, the hand was the same as his other flesh.

Now I heard God say to me, "Do as much," and I knew that the power He had given to Moses would now be mine.

So I put forth my hand and touched the leper on his breast and said no more than: "You will be clean."

His leprosy left him. He was clean. This was so great a miracle that I told him: "Say nothing to anyone."

But he went out and began to speak of his cure, and this caused such excitement that I knew it was time to go back to the desert before there was an inundation of lepers. Nor did I need the Lord to tell me that there might be grave obstacles to curing all of them, and all at once.

Indeed, it did seem true to me that the diseases of man were ranked like the angels. To cure the highest disease, which is but another way of saying the lowest, was to ask the Holy Spirit to descend by ten more dimensions into the pit. And I was weak from curing my first leper. Could it be that God might be diminished as well? It was by the aid of the Holy Spirit, after all, that I had brought forth my cures. And what was such a Spirit but the bond between my Father and myself?

I fled to the desert and told my followers that I would meet them in Capernaum.

19

For two nights I lay on the ground with snakes and scorpions and did my best to feel no fear. I would tell myself that John the Baptist could pick up a scorpion and talk to it and it did not sting, but I was not wholly successful. No scorpion stung me, yet I was afraid.

My return to Capernaum proved better. The first man to speak was a centurion standing before me in armor, and he had an eagle on his helmet. This Roman was proud; who could say how many he had killed with his sword? Yet he was also polite, saying, "Lord, my best servant is sick with palsy."

Without pause, I replied: "Let me come and heal him."

To increase my respect, the centurion gave a surprising reply: "Lord, I am not worthy for you to come under my roof. But if you will speak the word, my servant can be healed. I am a man to command a soldier to go and he will go. To another, I say 'Come,' and he comes. So my sick servant will do what needs to be done if you give me the power to tell him."

This centurion had tears in his eyes. I marveled at that, and turned to my followers: "Where have I found greater faith in anyone? Not in all of Galilee." And I said to the centurion, "Go! Your servant will be healed."

And he was. So others told me. By this I knew that if all was well, I could send God's power to others, even if they were not Jews. I felt elation at this, and was pleased by the acclaim of those who welcomed me on the streets. Many paused to greet me, and the mouths of such men were painted red. It was then that Simon Peter told me how Capernaum, though only a small city, was favored by men who did not know women but other men. So I also learned that such men would cover their lips with the juice of red berries, and in the taverns they would speak of how the bravest of the Greeks were Spartans, who were great warriors but lived only to sleep in each other's arms.

This brought forth a dispute among my fishermen, and Peter said: "Spartans also live with the sword. Whereas these men of Capernaum live with the coloring that women choose for their lips."

Nonetheless, I felt affection for my new followers. They

were tender in spirit, and would congregate beneath a tree, because they were not welcome in the temple. I was gentle with them.

In the synagogue, however, I spoke of the incarceration of John the Baptist in the dungeon of Machaerus. Since he was all but with me, I preached with the clarity that comes when no word must search for the next. And more men gathered each day at the synagogue, until there was no bench to receive them, not even in the vestibule or outside the door. One day four men tried to bring in a poor man who was paralyzed in every limb, but they could not come near the door because of the crowd. In desperation, these four men took a ladder and climbed to the roof, where they broke a hole between two rafters in order to lower the sick man (and his bed) down to where I spoke. I knew that if his bearers felt such concern for him, then the man must be worthy. Without pause I said: "Thy sins be forgiven thee." And he rose from his bed. I knew why. Those who came to me had undergone much torment and so were ready to recognize the weight of their sin. Thereby, they were ready to be cured. This paralyzed man had become equal in his suffering to the evil he had wrought, and so I could forgive him, and without hesitation.

The scribes were affronted. I heard one say, "Why does Jesus speak blasphemies? Who can forgive sins? God only."

I understood then that I was speaking too openly. Yet it

was difficult to be patient. The pious were becoming noxious now. The odor of their sanctity was close to the smell of shellfish when such creatures expire on the shore of the sea that once nourished them.

Therefore, when asked how I could dare forgive sins, I said: "Why seek to reason? The man was brought to me paralyzed, yet afterward he could carry his bed out of the synagogue; if he staggered, it was only by a little." So they were much offended.

Each day I came to understand a little more of why the Lord had chosen me. I could see how my Father's patience would be tried with His creation. We consumed His charity and kept repeating our sins. So He must need someone as simple as myself to listen to men's errors. Even as I had known a void in my heart while I fasted, so could I now comprehend those waste-places in the hearts of others where a good opinion of oneself cannot be kept, not even in contemplating one's good deeds. The soul can feel empty before the memory of its sins. How much compassion did I feel in that moment for those who sin! And I prayed that the Lord would always speak through me.

20

I began to see my need for disciples who would follow me every day and work at tasks where my ability was small. When I saw Levi sitting at the customshouse, I said: "Follow me," because he had a good and cunning face, and I had need of the light in his eye.

Levi came with us. Nor did I concern myself that he was a publican, a tax collector. But soon I learned that few men were as unpopular as those who worked in customshouses gathering taxes for Romans. All the same, I had but one measure for a sinner: Was there some promise of happiness in his countenance? Even a man who cheated others or worked for Romans could reveal more of God to me than I would find in those who were sinless but downcast.

Moreover, I had need of twelve men, one for each of the twelve tribes of Israel, twelve who could look back into my eyes and allow me to see what was in their hearts.

There was one for whom I could not say that, and he was Judas Iscariot. With his dark beard, he was handsome. I wished him to be among my twelve even if I could not see what was in his heart. His eyes were too full of fire. Indeed, I felt blinded by the blaze of his spirit. Notwithstanding, I welcomed him. He claimed to love the poor, saying that he had lived among the rich long enough to despise them. His father was rich, and Judas said that he knew the deceits of the powerful, and all their foul arts. So I knew that he could teach me much more, even though I had to wonder whether he might be Satan's gift to me. But I did not stay long with such a concern. Other matters pressed more.

I lived among those twelve men who were ready to follow me, and hoped that I could teach some of them how to cast out demons, for then I could send them forth to preach. To do that, however, they needed to come closer to me. I could rely on Simon Peter, but I could not as yet be as certain of the sons of Zebedee, James and John, nor of Andrew and Philip and Bartholomew and Thomas, and another named James, and Thaddeus, and Simon the Canaanite and Judas Iscariot, of whom I have spoken. He, I knew, could not be taught. He was too proud. Last of all was the publican Levi, who was also called Matthew, but since he was not the same Matthew who wrote a gospel, let him remain as Levi.

In choosing these disciples I aroused much dissatisfaction among the Pharisees. When I would eat meat in the house of Levi, many sinners also sat with us, and some were tax collectors. Heavy in their hearts that they worked for the Romans, they were full of shame before their fellow Jews. So they had need of me.

Yet when the scribes and Pharisees saw us eating together, they said: "How can he mingle with these dregs?" I was not eager to increase the absence of good feeling that existed already between these Pharisees of Capernaum and myself, so I answered: "They that are whole have no need of the physician. They that are sick need much. I am not here to call the righteous to repentance but the sinners."

I debated how to tell these Pharisees that sinners, having encountered the Evil Spirit, may even come to feel repugnance for their old appetites, whereas the pious think only of protecting themselves from the temptations of Satan, so they fester within.

Besides, I was happy to eat with sinners. Some of Levi's friends were unwashed (for Levi was loyal to poor friends), yet by coming to know such people, I began to wonder about the godlessness of many who were rich. They did not use their wealth to make others happy, whereas here, at the table of Levi, among these poor sinners, I saw how there might be much petty injury each could do to another, yet there was also much simple pity that they would feel for those beside them. So the faces of the poor at Levi's table had a dignity like the grain of unpolished wood after it has been exposed to the warmth and wrath of sun and rain.

I also knew that such an argument would hardly satisfy the Pharisees. They would say: "The disciples of John the Baptist fasted. Why don't your people do the same?" And so pious were their voices that at night I would brood over those Jews who spoke for my religion and drove away sinners.

But there were many questions for me. Why did I seek out men who would rather eat and drink than pray? Was it that those who boasted of how they were children of Abraham did not believe that more would be demanded of them than good attendance at the synagogue? I would tell myself that a feast was being prepared in heaven where the pious would be cast out. Only the poor and the sinful would be invited to the banquet. And with that I would drink my wine and wonder at how much I drank. In my family, wine had been reserved for solemn occasions. Now we drank at every meal.

These publicans were rarely solemn. Still, I trusted the good spirit between us. It was not a time to fast. There was much to prepare for the Lord. To fast would make us gloomy, and we would become like those who praise God with their words but remain so afraid of other men that they can never praise Him by bold deeds.

Such were my thoughts while drinking wine. I could bring salvation to sinners. But my head whirled with vertigo. There was so little time, and so many obstacles to foresee. What of the pagan who might seek baptism? Would he be ready to cast out his idols? Would his own family then cast him out?

These differences with the Pharisees of Capernaum were made worse when my publicans walked through the fields on the Sabbath and plucked ears of corn. The Pharisees said: "To harvest on this day is not lawful." And when I answered, my voice was in a race with my caution, yet my words gained the victory. I said: "The Sabbath was made for man, not man for the Sabbath."

On the next Sabbath, when I entered the synagogue a laborer was there and he had a withered hand. Many Pharisees, much aroused, watched to see if I would heal him. I could see that they were waiting to accuse me, so I thought to say no to this laborer.

As soon as he spoke, however, I was helpless. He said: "I used to be a stonemason, but then my fingers were smashed. I plead with you, Yeshua, give me back a good hand and then I will not have to beg for my family's food."

I could not refuse. I said to him: "Stand forth."

I asked of the congregation, "Is it lawful to do good on the Sabbath?"

No one could answer. They did not have the courage to

say "Cure him." The hardness of their hearts (and no heart is so hard as the timid heart) infuriated me. I spoke to the man, saying: "Stretch forth your hand," and when he did, I did not even have to touch it; at once I could see how his hand was restored as whole as the other. Yet I also felt anguish. Most of the Pharisees left in outrage. I had to conclude that a time might come when I would go to war with some of my own people.

Later that night, a Pharisee from the synagogue who knew an officer of Herod Antipas living in Capernaum told Peter that Herod was now considering whether this Yeshua of Nazareth ought to be stilled. I decided that I would do well to look for a cave on the shores of the Sea of Galilee. For Yeshua of Nazareth would not seem the Son of God to the officers of Herod, only a poor Jew.

21

Yet I was not alone. My disciples accompanied me, and with them came many others. The word had passed through the hills and valleys of Galilee, even into the mountains. I, however, did not feel ready to speak. My disciples were now obliged to comport themselves as soldiers and become my guard. Nonetheless, I could feel the desire of these people to touch me, and I gave way until they were too many and I lost the power to cure. Truth, their fingers so implored my flesh that I had to live with my own bruises when day was done.

I told my disciples to find a small ship and let it wait in a cove of the Sea of Galilee. Once on board I would be near shore but apart, and thereby could preach from the prow, only returning to land long enough to lay hands on a few.

While waiting, I went up onto a mountain. Many followed. I came down by another path to a town near Capernaum and entered a house where I was welcome. But another multitude surrounded this house. There were even two scribes from Jerusalem among them.

Before long I heard that one of these scribes had said to another, "Since he is the prince of devils, Beelzebub is able to cast out other devils." The danger I had been expecting was near. Even as I was earning more and more knowledge of how to cure, so was a plague of ill spirit spreading. The righteous could only see my efforts as the Devil's labor: For how could a modest man like me command miracles? Already many were saying that I was ready to deny the Ten Commandments and the myriad of laws surrounding them. Whereas they, good Pharisees, prayed for a world where all were law-abiding. So I knew that I must speak to the two scribes from Jerusalem. And when I looked into their eyes, I had hope; they appeared to be wise.

I said: "You compare me to Beelzebub. But if I am a demon who is able to destroy other demons, am I not also destroying myself? When Satan can cast out Satan, he has become a house divided. Do we not know that a kingdom divided against itself cannot stand?"

These scribes went away, their faces stern. Severity can also be the expression of those who have no reply.

It was a day of many ills. Two messengers came to this same house from John the Baptist. He had spoken to them while in the prison at Machaerus. Now they were furnished with questions to ask. "Are you the one who is to come?" was John's question. "Or am I to look for another?"

My disciples were distrustful of John's disciples. They said: "The Baptist is jealous of you."

I would not believe that. If John no longer said that I was the one to follow him, it was because he had heard I was consorting with sinners. In how much distrust must John now live! The walls of a dungeon weigh upon thought; they bend certainty. John might no longer know me. Could he understand that my power to work miracles was a sign that the Lord was not displeased that I sat at table with sinners? Could John not see that I was still his messenger? I said to the two people who had come from John: "The lame walk. Lepers are cleansed. Demons are driven out. Those with palsy no longer tremble. Blessed is any man who shall not be offended in me." And I sent these two messengers away. But among my own people, I defended John: "Among those who are born of women," I told them, "there has not risen a greater man than John the Baptist." Now, my disciples did not understand. They could only hear my words as a diminishment of myself.

Not even with all they had seen were my disciples certain who I might be.

To this same house now came my mother with my brothers, James and John. Standing outside, they called for me. But a multitude was all about and I did not hear them. Then one man cried: "Behold, your mother and your brothers look for you." I still did not reply. I had heard that my mother was arguing with my followers. She had said that I was wrong to perform cures on the Sabbath and so must be full of devils. My brothers said worse. They said that I was not of a proper mind. They had come to take me home. Indeed, I had always known that my brothers were jealous of me. So when the man cried out again, "Behold, your mother and your brothers look for you," I answered, "Who is my mother? Who are my brothers?" And I stared at all in the room as if I had need of every man and woman there. I said, "These are my brothers! Those who are with me. For he who does the will of God is my brother and my mother."

Later, I would hear that my mother wept when my words were repeated to her. How I wished to gather those words back. I owed much to her, even if our ways together had never been smooth. She had lived in so much fear. When I was young, she had made me afraid of Romans, too afraid. And she was lacking in pride when she spoke to wealthy Jews; she felt they were more important than herself. All of this had served to feed my anger.

22

In the evening, being not without remorse at what I had said about my mother, I felt a need to go to the sea and said to my disciples, "Let us pass over to the other side."

Now, they had been feasting in every house that welcomed us. They had certainly noticed that the rich in these towns around Capernaum were often ready to receive us. So my disciples ate well and drank much and had few cares. But I needed peace.

In these weeks many sick people had been conducted to me, and many who were mad; also those with sore limbs. I had tried to heal them all. And when the Holy Spirit passed from my heart to my hand, one touch could make them well.

Yet at such times I would recall the leap I had not taken on the invitation of the Devil. Now, even as the grace of healing passed from my hand into the body of whoever was before me, I could still feel the mark of cowardice on my own flesh. For it is cowardly to fear death as I had feared it. Now I would make amends by recalling my shame. That was just. I would not be proud of my good deeds. I would brood upon my hour with the Devil. Had I given some of my fealty to him?

Such sentiments would return whenever I found people whom I could not cure. I saw darkness in their eyes, and that could make them seem like angels of Satan. I knew I had need again of the sea, or of a lake as large as the Sea of Galilee, so that I could free my breath of thoughts as heavy as these.

I told my closest followers to send away our multitudes. By evening, when most were gone, we walked quickly to a ship; still there were some who followed and embarked after us in smaller ships. Whereupon a great wind swept across the water.

The waves beat upon our vessel. Some washed over the bow. If others were terrified, I knew nothing of their panic. I was sleeping peacefully. Such peace had been given to me by the rocking of the ship. Yet when my disciples awakened me, it was to say, "Many boats are about to founder. Master, do you care if we perish?"

So I said to the wind, "Be still." And soon there was

calm. In truth, I do not know if I can say that this miracle was mine. Even on awakening I could sense that the end of the storm was near. Yet I was pleased to say: "Why are you all so fearful? Have you no faith?"

I could hear them, one to another, saying: "Who is this man? Even the seas obey him."

Now, the wharf where we landed was in the country of the Gadarenes near the shores of Decapolis, a pagan city in the land of the gentiles. I was not easy. This was neither our land nor friendly, and we had come to a beach beneath high cliffs containing many tombs.

From one of these tombs descended a giant, and he was carrying a torch. His spirit was so unclean that the fire of the torch blazed fiercely with the force of his breath. Quickly, he came toward me. No one of my followers, not even Peter, was ready to resist this man, for as all could see, he was a son of the Nephilim, the fallen ones. His ancestors had been angels who lusted after women and fathered children who grew into giants. These pagans, huge men, brought carnage and disorder to everyone.

Yet even as I said, "Peace," he stopped.

Having stopped, he said, "No man can bind me. No man can command me."

"Then of what are you afraid?"

"Of all things," he replied. "I live in the darkness of these tombs, and I weep. With sharp stones I cut my flesh. But of you I have heard. I worship you."

"What have you heard?" I asked.

"That your eyes have a great light," he said, "and your name is Jesus. Or so I have heard from those who dare to speak to me." And by the trembling of his lips I saw that he was ready to call upon his strength but only in the name of blind strength.

"Many speak in terror of who I am," he said. "I contain more devils than any other. I adjure thee: Torment me not, Jesus! I give warning."

I was not without fear; this man was as powerful as a large bull. Moreover, the fellow was filthy. His hair grew into his beard, and his locks were like the fardes of thick rope that hold a ship to its mooring.

He said: "I live in the tombs of those who are damned."

"What is your name?"

He answered: "My name is Legion. We are many, and the sum of this many are in me."

I knew he was filled with devils—so many that they might be too much for me. Yet the hand of the Lord was on my back and urging me forward. "The unclean spirits who devoured King Herod are now in you," I said. "Flee from Legion. Flee." And I growled like a beast, which is what the Essenes do to enforce a commandment they receive from the Lord. And as I growled, so did a great herd of wild swine come rushing from the field beneath the tombs, and a turmoil of devils issued from the throat of Legion. How they screamed! I heard: "Let us in! Let us into the swine of Gadarene." A demon must inhabit a body. Whereupon I let them enter the herd, and they rushed with a great noise into these swine, who, upon receiving them, ran violently down a gorge into the sea. The number of these beasts was two thousand, and they all drowned, all the swine of Gadarene. Even these low animals could not bear such foul invaders.

Others soon came forward to look at a man who had been possessed by so many devils. But now they found Legion clothed and bathed and in good spirit. No matter. The elders from the town of Gadarene were afraid. They entreated me to quit their shore.

Yet as I returned to my ship, Legion began to beg that I let him come with my people. I was tempted. He would make a mighty apostle. But their number was twelve, and I could not add another. Moreover, he was a pagan. Still I could take no pride in saying: "Go instead to your people and tell them what happened." In truth, I abhorred the man. The rush of those demons who came out of his throat had been unfathomable in its uproar. Who could vouch for the cause of such a misery?

After he left, Legion spoke well of me among the gentiles in the city of Decapolis, where he went to live. They marveled at his words of praise. In former days, he had never had a good word for any man.

23

On my return to Capernaum, one of the elders of the synagogue (his name was Jairus) stepped forward and knelt at my feet. Until now, not one of the Pharisees had offered more than a place to teach (and this grudgingly). Yet here was Jairus. He pleaded with me, saying, "My little daughter lies near death. I pray thee, come and heal her so that she may live."

By now I had learned how close was faith to the loss of faith. Both stole silently into the heart. So I understood: The rulers of the synagogue might disapprove of me, but that did not mean I had failed to enter their hearts. Much strengthened, then, by this meeting, I went with Jairus to his house, and a horde came with us. As we passed through the street, I knew that someone had done me an ill. All virtue had suddenly left me. I turned and said, "Who touched my clothes?"

A stranger said: "You see the multitude, yet you ask 'Who touched me?'" But then a woman cried out and fell down before us. "I have had an issue of blood for twelve years," she said, "and have spent all I own on physicians and have only grown worse. Hearing of you, I touched your garment. I thought: 'That shall make me whole.' And it did. I have stopped bleeding."

I could see by her eyes that she spoke the truth. So I was gentle. I told her, "Daughter, go in peace and you will be wholly healed by tomorrow." No sooner had she left, however, than a servant from the house of Jairus came to him and said, "Your daughter lives no longer."

Had the ailing woman taken the virtue I had been gathering to save the child?

But in that instant my Father was with me, and feeling His strength, I turned to this ruler of the synagogue and said, "Jairus, be not afraid. Only believe." I had to hope that the daughter was not dead but resting in that long shadow of sleep that is near to death. For then I might save her. I did not know if I had the power to bring back those who are truly dead.

I recited to myself the words of the prophet Isaiah: "Awake and sing, ye that dwell in dust."

At the house of Jairus there was much disturbance. Many were weeping and wailing. I entered and said: "The girl is not dead but sleeps."

And I spoke in this manner to calm the air. The dead are best raised in silence; tumult can only drive them further away. So I asked the mourners to leave the house and went with Jairus and his wife to where their daughter was lying. I held her hand and recited words I remembered well from the scroll of the Second Kings, saying: " 'When Elisha was come into the house, behold, the child was dead, and he prayed unto the Lord. And he lay upon the child and put his mouth upon the child's mouth and his eyes upon the child's eyes and his hands over the boy's hands, and he stretched himself upon the child and the flesh of the child was now warm, and the child sneezed seven times and opened his eyes.'

"And this," I told the father and mother, "having been spoken, need not be done again." For I knew that if I lay upon the girl and she failed to stir, incalculable would be the harm. With the power of the Lord in my hand, I merely touched her and said, "Good daughter, unto thee I say arise." And straightaway she arose and walked. Her parents were astonished, but I told them to give her food, and give it with all the love that they possessed, and this I said because the child, half awake, seemed full of misery that she had returned to the living. Nor did I know whether she had actually died and come back. But I did understand that much unhappiness between husband and wife had laid a pall upon the girl. I could see that she lived in a house of many unclean feelings. No air was sweet in these rooms, and those stale miseries that feed upon themselves were with us. Before I left, I told Jairus and his wife to fast, to pray, and to leave a flower each morning in a small jar by the child's bed.

It had been simple when I told the girl to rise, but there was a weight on me. Much had been drained from my limbs by the woman who touched my garment, and more now by arousing this child who barely wished to live. Had I drawn too deeply upon the powers of the Lord? Would it have been wiser to save His efforts for other matters? I felt a desire to return to Nazareth, and knew I wanted to apologize to my mother for that hour when I had wounded her love.

24

So I went back to my own country, and my disciples followed, and in Nazareth I spent two days with Mary. Yet I do not know if I soothed her feelings, for how could she forgive me after I had said: "Who is my mother?"

On the Sabbath, I began to teach in the synagogue, but it was not long before I heard sounds of discontent. Soon people were saying, "What wisdom is this?" And when I told them of my works, of the leper and of the storm, I felt a loss of modesty (which loss was now like a foul spirit in me). Moreover, I was not believed. It was as if word had traveled everywhere but to Nazareth. I could hear them say, "Isn't this the carpenter, the son of Mary?" And I won-

dered if any blow to pride wounds more than the obliga-
tion to honor a man who has been no larger than oneself
until this hour. I was pained that they would offer me no
love. "A prophet is without honor in his own country and
among his own kin and in his own house," I said. "Nor
can a doctor cure anyone who knows him. Of course, a
doctor is no better than his patient." And indeed in
Nazareth I could do no mighty work.

Still, there came the next Sabbath, and again I awoke
with the strength of my Father, and was able to cure a
woman who had lived with an infirmity for eighteen
years. Yet I was scolded before evening by another ruler
of this small temple for healing on the Sabbath day. He
was a rich man, much pleased with himself, and he said:
"There are six days on which men are to work and in such
days they can be healed, not on the Sabbath."

To which I answered, "You let your ox out of the stall on
the Sabbath and lead him to water. Yet you do not allow
this woman to be loosed from her bonds on the day we
celebrate the works of the Lord."

But he was more than ready for debate. He replied:
"Some of us do not loose our oxen on the Sabbath. Faith
is a narrow road." This offended me. I should have said:
"Hypocrite! You do lead your ox to water on the Sabbath.
You do not want him to thirst and lose value." But I was
prudent and said: "Narrow is the way that leads unto life,
and the way to destruction is broad."

He nodded, as if he were the one who would now come closer to the sweetmeat of the question: "The broad highway of simple faith is without peril," he said, "on days that are fair. When it rains or it is night, such breadth in the road turns into a trackless mire. Seek ye, Yeshua, for the narrow path that mounts between the rocks. Do not look for cures on the Sabbath. That is the broad highway."

With this, he laid his hand on my shoulder as if he were fatherly and I was of lesser faith. In the touch of his fingers was all the confidence of a wealthy man. His hand said to my flesh: "Respect my words. Much position rests beneath."

He had shamed me. My powers left. Once again, and in my own synagogue, I was without strength.

25

As soon as I left Nazareth, however, some good spirits returned concerning all that we could do. Indeed the time had come to send messengers forth. Nor did I think it unlikely that they would be able to perform acts like mine. Word of my power to heal had spread among many, and so many might be ready to have faith in my apostles.

I told them to go on their journey with nothing but a staff; no bread, no money, only one coat. I said: "Wherever you enter into a house, abide there until you depart. Whoever does not receive you, leave him quickly. Shake the dust from your feet. By so moving you will go your way with ease."

I also knew that I could give my disciples a part of what the Lord had bestowed on me only if I did not rest in my labors and never felt sorrow for myself: The destruction of each man is to be found in the pity he saves for himself. This was twice true for the Son of the Lord. So would it also be twice true for his closest followers.

I told them of other things. Indeed, there was much to learn. In a short time. So my speech was harsh. I was coming to understand that to repent of one's sins generates turmoil in a man; the soul races to and fro. That is the time when a gentle word may not be wise. If too distracted, we do not hear it.

I also told them not to worry if there were matters they did not understand. They still knew enough to teach others. "What you hear," I told them, "is the wisdom of the Lord. This you may preach from the housetops. Never fear those who can kill the body but are not able to kill the soul. Instead, fear God. He can destroy both soul and body. For, remember: God knows everything. Not one sparrow can fall to the ground without your Father's knowledge. Fear not, therefore. You are worth more than many sparrows."

What I said next did not come easily to my tongue. It was prideful. Nonetheless, these were the words chosen by the Lord, and so they were in my mouth: "Whoever denies me, I will deny before my Father." Some of the apostles drew back. They knew that they had not been ready to tell everyone they met that they were of my co-hort.

I looked into the eyes of each of the twelve and said: "I have come not to send peace but a sword." And this was different from all I had said before. I had come to bring peace on earth, but now the Lord had given me a vision of many battles and they would all take place before peace could come. And my heart was sore with the pain that I had not made peace with Mary when I was last in Nazareth. So I spoke not only with the Lord's anger but with my own. My family had left me divided. So I said: "A man's foes can be the members of his own household. Whoever would love father or mother more than me is not worthy of me, just as he who would find his life must first lose it. Yet he who loses his life for my sake shall find it."

Now my apostles were weeping. No thought arouses more compassion for oneself than the belief that one is losing one's life for a friend; at such an instant one feels noble. It is natural to mourn for oneself. So I tried to teach them what is to be found in the laws of love, for such laws are much concealed. I said: "Love your friends like your own soul. Guard them like the pupil of your eye. Be glad only when you can look at them with love. Know that no crime is more onerous than to sadden your brother's spirit."

With this, they sighed. They saw the truth of what I had said; they also saw its difficulty.

With those words I sent them out to preach.

Now, I chose to live alone in a hut abandoned by shepherds, high in the hills above Capernaum. And I tried to
subdue the fears that still remained with me.

Each fear was terrible. Each came upon me in the mid-
dle of the night. My limbs were heavy, and no road appeared.

26

The first of these fears was the worst. Nor was it a dream. I had learned that John the Baptist was dead. He had been slain in his dungeon at Machaerus, and it was King Herod Antipas who commanded the deed.

For so long as I had known of John's imprisonment I had believed that God would set him free. Now I knew that the firmest of my beliefs could be in error—I was like a man whose foot has slipped on the edge of a cliff.

A second fear followed the first. Many were already saying that John had risen from the dead. He was bringing forth mighty works and miracles. Some were ready to believe that John and Jesus were one. The peril was clear. If

Herod Antipas had slain John the Baptist once, he might not fail to kill him again. The way of John's death was a scourge to my sleep.

My disciples had told me how it came about. They had heard much, and from many: Herod first imprisoned John as punishment for saying: "It is not lawful for you to take your dead brother's wife." Lady Herodias, once married to Philip, the brother, was now wed to Herod Antipas. Having heard those words, Herodias, the new wife, reviled John's name. Then she reviled Herod Antipas. He had not punished John. Finally, the king ordered his guard to arrest the preacher. A monarch is weak before the righteous wrath of a queen who is without righteousness.

Yet Herodias could not convince Herod Antipas to name a day when the Baptist would be executed. The king still feared such an act. Who knew what powers God had given to John?

On the birthday of Herod Antipas, a feast was prepared in the fortress of Machaerus. Before all of the lords and high captains, Salome, the daughter of Herodias and the dead brother, now danced. Salome danced so ardently that Herod Antipas put her in a seat of honor beside him. Then he said: "Ask of me what you will. I will give it." Salome replied that his words were without weight. They had been promised to the air and only to the air.

Herod Antipas now gave his vow: "Whatever you ask

for, I will give, even if you ask for half of my kingdom. That is my oath."

A king's oath weighs as much as the keel of the ship that he builds for his soul; his oath strengthens him. To break such a vow would leave him damned by the filth of his own deeds and the bloody misdeeds of his servants.

When Salome told her mother what the king had promised, Herodias said, "Ask for the head of John the Baptist."

Herod Antipas honored his oath. In that hour, he sent for an executioner and ordered the head of John to be brought to him. And when it was carried into the banquet room, Herod Antipas gave it to Salome. She is said to have placed it on a silver platter and then danced with it before Herod's guests.

I did not often sleep. Alone in my cave, I looked for solace in the thought that God was near while Herod Antipas was in his palace and far away.

In the darkness I wept. John's way had been hard. He never drank wine, yet many said that he had a devil; now of me, what would they say? "A drunkard and a glutton. A devil equal to Beelzebub." My apostles would meet many who would not listen to them.

27

There came the day when they returned. They were woeful as they spoke of their attempts to cure others. They asked me often: "Why could we not cast out devils? All things should be possible to him who believes."

I told them that even when one prayed for one's faith to be perfect, a portion of oneself remained without faith. "I asked a man once if he could believe. He answered, 'Lord, I believe. Help me in my disbelief.' This," I told them, "is wisdom!"

My disciples were still gloomy. They had failed to cure the sick.

I decided to embark again with them on the Sea of Galilee. Boats could always be found for us by Levi, who knew many ship owners who wished to please him since he counted their taxes. So we were soon able to escape our followers for a few hours. Yet some people saw us departing and followed on foot around the empty shore. When we landed and went up into a mountain, they continued to follow.

I had been weary from loss of sleep when we set out, but now I was moved with compassion and was ready to teach once more. How could I not? I knew every error I had made. My throng were like sheep without a shepherd, and I had given them quick hope that they could perform cures. But they did not love my Father enough. I should have known that. But then, I did not love Him enough, not enough. I had not trusted Him with the same whole faith that I asked my followers to offer. I must put away, therefore, all doubt. I must convince all who listened of my love for Him. And so, full of the loss of John the Baptist, I taught for most of that day on the mountain.

Later, those who became my scribes, and most notably Matthew, in his gospel, would speak of my Sermon on the Mount. They had me saying all manner of things, and some were the opposite of others. Matthew put so many sayings together, indeed, that he might as well have had me not ceasing to speak for a day and a night, and speaking out of two mouths that did not listen to each other. I can only recount what I know: I wished to bring all of them to my knowledge of God.

I was beginning to understand how large was the task.

I could not carry the Lord's message by myself. Too many would oppose me. I needed an army of apostles. If each of my twelve would be able to find his own twelve, and each of these new apostles were to bring to us another twelve, I would have an army. So I knew that I must send my apostles out again, to return with their own disciples.

Yet large armies bring discord. If faith was simple for some, it would soon be a labyrinth for the Son of Man; at each turning I would soon wonder whether I was closer to the light or had drawn nearer to darkness. And it may be that for this reason (my faith still remaining simple to me) I spoke with much conviction on this day and was full of admiration for my Father's works. Indeed, I was now confident that His love was ready to forgive all who would come to Him. So I sought to move them to love of God rather than to adoration of my cures. My words rang out on the mountain.

"Blessed are the poor in spirit," I told them on this day, "for theirs is the Kingdom of Heaven. Blessed are they that mourn, for they shall be comforted. Blessed are the meek; they shall inherit the earth." And saying this, so too did I believe it.

"Blessed are those who thirst after righteousness," I said, "for they shall be filled. And blessed are the merciful; they shall obtain mercy. Blessed are the pure in heart. For they shall see God."

I felt hope in all who listened, and its rising was as visible to me as the gathering of the dawn. So I spoke of light. I told them: "You are the light of the world. A city that is set on a hill cannot be hid. Neither do men light a candle and put it under a bushel, but on a candlestick and then it gives light to all who are in the house."

And if I would bring them to greater love, I knew that I must also use words that they would not wish to hear, and would have trouble believing, even as I had trouble believing. The desire for revenge was not only in the marrow of their souls but in mine. Yet if I would love God in such a way that they also could love Him, then they must believe in Him as I did at this moment. So I said what they could hardly bear to hear:

"If someone," I said, "shall strike you on your right cheek, turn to him the other cheek. And if a man will take your coat, give him your cloak as well." I could feel the desperation with which they sought to understand this, to believe this. "You have heard it said," I told them, "that you shall love your neighbor and hate your enemy. But I say: Love your enemy. Bless him who curses you. Do good to those that hate you. Pray for them who persecute you. Then, and only then, can you become the children of your Father. For He makes His sun to rise upon the evil and on the good, and He sends rain on the just and on the unjust. If you only love those who love you, what reward do you have? Be perfect, therefore, even as your Father in Heaven is perfect." And I knew that they, like me, had a great desire to believe this.

For that reason, I sought to explain how His generosity

was mighty: "Take no thought for your life, nor for what you shall eat or what you shall drink, nor yet for your body, nor for what you shall put on. Is life not more than meat? And the body more than raiment? The fowls of the air do not sow, neither do they reap. Yet your heavenly Father feeds them. Consider the lilies of the field: They toil not, neither do they spin, and yet even Solomon in all his glory was not arrayed like one of them. If God so clothed the grass of the field, shall He not clothe you? Therefore, take no thought to go about, saying, 'What shall we eat?' or 'What shall we drink?' or 'Where shall we be clothed?' For your heavenly Father knows that you have need of all these things. Seek first the Kingdom of God and His righteousness, and all these things shall be added unto you. Take, then, no thought for the morrow; tomorrow will take thought for itself. Sufficient unto the day is the evil thereof."

And I said to them: "Let us all pray together," and as I heard their voices repeating my words, I felt as mighty as Leviathan rising from the deep.

Together we prayed:

"Our Father, who art in heaven,
Hallowed be Thy name.
Thy Kingdom come,
Thy will be done
In earth as it is in heaven.

Give us this day our daily bread,
And forgive us our trespasses, as we forgive those who
trespass against us.
And lead us not into temptation
But deliver us from evil.
For Thine is the Kingdom and the power and the glory
forever.
Amen."

And I said "Amen" many times as we descended from the mountain. It was late in the day. My disciples said, "It would be wise to send them away now. They must go back into their villages and buy bread, for they have nothing to eat and here is a desert."

But to send them away was not in my thoughts. These people had walked over sharp stones to join us and they had listened to me. And I could still feel the Lord's hand at my elbow. I said: "Give them to eat."

My disciples said: "You are the one who must provide. Did you not say to us: 'Take no thought of: "What shall we eat?" or "What shall we drink?" ' "

I had said it.

"How many loaves have we?" I asked.

They looked. There were five barley loaves and two dried fish. So I told the disciples to seat all our followers in companies upon the ground. And I took those five loaves and divided them exceedingly small, until there were a hundred pieces of bread from each loaf. Then the two fish gave up more than twice two hundred small morsels. And, with five hundred bits of bread and five hundred of fish, I passed these morsels to each of the followers, doing it myself for all five hundred. I would lay one flake of fish and one bit of bread upon each tongue. Yet when each person had tasted these fragments, so do I believe that each morsel became enlarged within his thoughts (even as once in Cana I had been enlarged by eating one grape), and so I knew that few among these hundreds would say that they had not been given sufficient fish and bread. And this was a triumph of the Spirit rather than an enlargement of matter. Which for the Lord is but a small deed, considering that He made the heavens and the earth out of nothing, and could certainly have changed our five loaves into five hundred.

Later, this story was much exaggerated by Mark and Matthew and Luke. No angel appeared in the sky, nor did the manna that God gave to Moses appear. But such was the power of the blessing of the Lord that my followers were satisfied. I felt as if I were a carpenter's apprentice again and had gathered with my fellows in a green field (rather than on the stones of a desert beach). We were eating with much joy. Indeed, it was a feast. Perhaps that is why Mark gave me not less than five thousand loaves and hundreds of fish and burdened my disciples with twelve baskets of food to bear home. Whereas we were five hundred, and brought nothing back but ourselves.

Exaggeration is the language of the Devil, and no man is free of Satan, not even the Son of God (and certainly not Matthew, Mark, Luke, or John). So I knew that many of my followers would increase the numbers of this feat. Yet I also suspected that my Father preferred each miracle to equal no more than the need that called it forth. Even as waste will exist in all matters, so in the working of miracles, extravagance is best avoided. And by that, I believed I now understood my Father.

But it was not for me to understand Him. Not every one of my miracles would be so modest. A little later, after I debarked again with my disciples, we rowed to Bethsaida, on the other side of this Sea of Galilee.

As we came to land, I told them all to sleep on the ship. I would go ashore by myself. I wished only to satisfy my desire to meditate upon the events of this fine day.

As night came, a gale arose. From where I sat, high on the shore, I could see that our ship was tossed by waves. So I came down again to the water and began to swim to the boat. Of a sudden, I was up and above the waters! I was walking! And I could even hear my Father's laughter at my pleasure in walking upon His water. Then came a second wave of His laughter. He was mocking me. For I had concluded too quickly that there was no extravagance in His miracles. I had forgotten how in the Book of Job, our Lord had trampled upon the back of the sea. I, walking now upon water (if with a gentle step), thought of how my Father had spoken to Job out of the whirlwind and told him: "Here shall the proud waves be stayed," yes, and He had "entered into the springs of the sea" and He had "walked in search of the depth." When young, I had read these words many times, and now the waves beneath my feet had become a path. And God was joyful at my admiration. For now I knew the true extent of His domain. He had lived before the day was born or the water stirred or the earth formed. He had brought my seed from the east and He had gathered me from the west and He controlled the waters of chaos. And I was joyful for such a vision, and did not want my joy to end. I was going to continue walking right past the boat of my disciples. But I didn't. I stopped instead to look at them. And they were frightened. Who could be striding beside them? I heard many cry out. One said, "It is a ghost!" I said, "Have courage. It is I. I am." Which is to say that I was not a spirit. And added, "Be not afraid."

Peter now said, "Lord, if it is you, ask me to come to you."

"Come."

Peter stepped out of the ship. We both thought that he too could walk. But the wind was wild. He sank. "Lord, save me!" he cried.

I stretched out my hand and caught him and said: "Why did you doubt?" And went back into the boat with him.

It was then I knew that Peter wanted to be loyal. Yet I also knew that there would come a time when he would have to fail me. For his faith was in his mouth, not his legs. Never would men's sentiments reveal the presence of the Lord. He would only appear in their deeds. That was just! For the Devil, having learned the arts of speech from the Lord, could utter glorious phrases worthy of the Lord and stirring to the heart, even if nothing that was good in his words could last.

When Peter and I returned to the ship, my disciples asked: "Are you the Son of the Highest?"

Now, they had asked this many times before and each time I heard in their voices something that told me they were ready to believe. Still I also heard how they did not yet believe. With each day they might come closer, but not completely, not yet. So I understood that as much as they wished to be loyal, they might also fail me. In the presence of my great joy on this night—and I was feeling great joy at having come so close to my Father—their hearts would harden. For they could not share my wonder.

28

After our night at sea, we came ashore in the land of Genessaret and multitudes once more awaited us. When we entered a village, the afflicted lay on the street awaiting our visit.

By midday, I was weary; by evening, low; my garment was imbued with entreaties. And when I went to the synagogue, Pharisees were there from Jerusalem, and scribes among them. It was not long before they wished to speak.

They told me that they had seen my disciples eat bread with unclean hands. The publicans, sitting in each village square, had been collecting taxes for the Romans and had handled coins from early morning until they were done, then they gambled at night with the coins they kept for themselves. How could their hands not be filthy? But the Pharisees, when they come home from the market, do not eat unless they wash.

Yet one cannot honor the pious. For no matter what care is taken to satisfy them by studious observance of the laws, they can never be satisfied. Indeed, how can one obey the Law absolutely? The laws of observance were written by men more pious than oneself. Therefore the Law, if by a tittle, has once more been broken. One has failed again. So I stood before the Pharisees in the synagogue and spoke to them like a physician, saying: "There is nothing that can enter a man and defile him. It is only the things that come out of a man. Those who have ears to hear, let them hear."

Much low and unhappy murmuring came back to me from these Pharisees. Within the synagogue, in the presence of the altar, I was speaking of the natural uncleanliness of man, who, as he lives, must pollute. My words were offensive to the altar.

But I was speaking as well to my followers, and I did not cease: "What enters from without does not pass into a man's heart but into his belly, and goes out again into the drain." And they heard me whisper to myself, "That dirt which is on a man's hands is nothing." Now, I said aloud, "What comes out of a man, however, can defile him. From a man's heart issue evil thoughts, adulteries, fornications, murders, thefts, covetousness, wickedness, deceit, blasphemy, pride, even the evil eye."

My indignation mounted until I could not go on. Such a sudden fury had arisen in me that it took my breath away. These Pharisees scolded others for not washing when they did not know the sum of their own evil. Of course, they were terrified of evil from without! They were terrified even of the dust of the road and the mud of the fields. For as they saw it—and only in this manner could they see—it took no more than one mote of non-observance to unbalance the scales within. Dirt, to them, was a sea of sin. But where in any one of them could one find a love of God that was ready to sacrifice all that they had?

I left the synagogue. Before the night was done I had even cured a man who was deaf and had an impediment in his speech. This was done by no more than putting my fingers in his ears, whereupon he spit; then I touched his tongue, causing him to look up to heaven and sigh. With that I said: "Be opened." His ears opened, and the string of his tongue was loosed; he spoke. I smiled. For now the Pharisees would have to say (and their speech would be most elevated): "He obeyeth not the law of washing, but he maketh the deaf to hear and the dumb to speak."

On another occasion when I had been followed to another wasteland of the desert where I had hoped to retire for the day, again there was nothing to eat. This time we had seven loaves, and again I broke them into pieces and gave them to my disciples, who passed them on, rank on rank, file on file, and all were satisfied.

But those hours on the mountain when I had given my sermon were no longer near to me. On that day I had not spoken to my people with words that the Lord offered my tongue—no, I had declared my love for Him, and so the words had been mine. Now life was filled again with duty. For that reason, I would suppose, I had many thoughts concerning Moses. He had had to listen to the children of Israel weeping in the wilderness. His followers had said to him, "Who shall feed us? We remember the fish we had in Egypt, the cucumbers and the melons, the leeks, the onions, and the garlic. But now our soul is dried away." And no one of these children of Israel had been pleased with the manna God sent down. They had gathered it and pounded it and baked it in ovens and made cakes of it; but it tasted like oil of coriander. Every man was lamenting at the door of his tent. Even Moses was displeased. He said to the Lord, "Why have You laid the burden of all these people on me? Have I begotten them? It is too heavy for me."

And Moses asked the Lord to let him die, for his life was misery.

The Lord said, "Your people shall eat until this food comes out of their nostrils and is loathsome to them."

And by now I had a full understanding of why Moses was exhausted. Fatigue of the spirit is like a twisting of the limbs; new pain enters into the old.

One day, on the road to Bethsaida a blind man was brought to me at the gate; I took him by the hand and led him out of the town so that no one would witness the cure.

And when I had spit on his eyes and put my unwashed hands upon him, I asked what he saw.

He looked up and said, "I see men who look like trees that are walking."

I replied, "That is because men, like trees, bear a fruit of good and evil."

Then I put my hands on his eyes again, and he was wholly restored and saw every man clearly. I sent him away to his house and told him not to speak of it (although I knew he would), but I was not certain how long I could go on with these cures without exhausting myself. I was coming to believe that God, at the cost of supporting me, might be suffering His own weariness. But this thought I did not care to say even to myself.

There were nights when I would awaken and not know who I was. Once, passing through the town of Caesarea Philippi, I asked my disciples: "Who do they say I am?"

And some answered that I was said to be John the Baptist. Others spoke of Elijah. Still others told me: "They do not know, but think you are one of the old prophets."

And I said, and my heart was pounding: "But who do you say I am?"

And Peter—it may be that he was thinking of how I had

walked upon the water—asked gently: "Can one say that you are the Christ?"

Since I felt like an ordinary man in all ways but one, I could love Peter for the strength that his conviction gave me. Now I knew with more certainty than before that I must be the Son of God. Yet how could I be certain of that if no man recognized me?

29

I was coming to comprehend that one must enter the darkness that lives beneath every radiance of spirit. And I wished to open my apostles to such a truth. I told them of a dream that had visited me each night for seven nights; it was a dream that the Son of Man would go to Jerusalem and be denied by the High Priest and be crucified.

On hearing it, my disciples said, "No, you will live forever. And we will live with you."

Then I knew why darkness lies close to exaltation. If they loved me, it was for my power to work miracles, not because I might teach them to love others. They wished to preach like me, but only to increase their own power, not to preach with love. So I rebuked them, saying: "You savor not the things that be of God but the things that be of men." In the silence that followed these words, the dream was upon me again.

"If I am killed, I will rise again after three days," I said. But I did not know if I spoke the truth.

I looked into their eyes to see if their souls were open. For at just this moment, the miracle of faith would be present or would not. In their eyes I saw no more than a heaviness of spirit. It was the heaviness that speaks of concern for oneself. I had wanted to drive them toward faith, but now I realized that I, too, was not acting out of love for others but was looking for power to convince them. So I sighed at the intricacy of the heart. And they sighed after me, as if we all knew how close we had come to truth yet also knew how far away we were.

On another day, not long after, I wanted to be close to Peter and to James and to John. Had I not begun my ministry with them? So I chose to lead them up into a high mountain, and we were there by ourselves. A cloud followed. And I knew that a cloud like this had been overhead in the hour when Moses raised his tabernacle on Mount Sinai, and the cloud had descended to cover the altar.

In that time, the children of Israel had been in the desert for forty years. At each place where the cloud came to rest, they had pitched their tents. And they only moved when a stirring of the cloud told them to take up their journey again.

Here were we, at rest beneath another cloud, and Peter said, "Master, let us make three tabernacles: for you, for Moses, and for Elijah."

Straightaway, he built them. The cloud above us did not move, and the sky was without sun. Yet my raiment was shining. It seemed to be as brilliant as the light that must surround the souls of the just. Then I saw Elijah. He was standing beside me. Next to him was Moses.

I said to my three apostles, "What do you see?"

Peter answered, "I see nothing; he who sees God will surely die."

At that moment a flame rose from the first tabernacle, and Peter said: "You are the Christ."

I shook my head. Even at this moment, I could not be certain. Once more I told Peter of my dream: I must go into Jerusalem, and there I would die. But how could death come to the Son of the Lord of Jerusalem?

Peter said: "Put it far from thee, Lord." He would not accept my dream. If Satan could disguise himself as an angel of light, why could he not also come before me as Peter? So I said to him, "Get thee behind me, Satan."

Tears came to his eyes. I knew then that I still felt a great urge to come closer to these apostles. And of them all, Peter would be the first. I wanted Peter to know the beauty that was in his soul. As I thought this, the power of God rose in me and the terror of my dream was lessened.

Yet I could not keep the Lord's power for long. As we walked down the mountain, Peter and James and John fell into dispute on who would become the greatest among them. Perhaps they believed my dream after all and so were thinking of who could replace me. I was silent until we returned to Capernaum. Then I gathered my twelve and said: "If any of you is filled with the desire to be first, know that he shall be last."

At that moment, as if I had called for a fine example to show just such a difference, a young man came up to us and knelt before my feet and asked, "Good Master, what shall I do? How may I inherit eternal life? I have observed all the Commandments from my youth."

In his eyes I saw that he had a desire to please, and so I said (and this was also uttered for my apostles): "Sell what you have, and give to the poor. Then you will have treasure in heaven."

But the young man was not happy; he confessed that he had many possessions and was loath to lose them. I said: "Many sons and daughters of Abraham are living in filth and dying of hunger. Your house is full. How much goes to them?"

He went away.

I remarked to my disciples, "How hard it is for the rich to enter the Kingdom of Heaven!" But some of my people now murmured unhappily. I said: "Children, it is painful to trust in riches. You will learn that it is easier to pass a knot through the eye of a needle than for a rich man to enter the Kingdom of Heaven." They were astonished, saying among themselves, "Who, then, can be saved?" And one of them, whose face was hidden by the others, muttered, "God enriches those He trusts. Why else is there high regard for wealth?" Another said, "If not the rich, who can be saved?"

I said, "No man can be saved if he counts his money." At which point Peter would remind me: "We have left everyone to follow you."

Now I had to tell myself that my disciples were but men, and lived among small passions; they were no better, and no worse, than other men. All the same, this dispute among my apostles over who came first had left me rigid with wrath. I said to them: "Forgive us our debts as we forgive our debtors." They did not hear the mockery in my voice.

No, they liked this saying. Had I discovered the largest passion among my men? To be forgiven their debts? It was clear that they would not be equally forgiving to the debts owed them.

I had been looking for an army of men whose souls were so pure that they would need no swords. Instead, I had gathered a few followers who argued among themselves over who would sit to the right of me and who would be first when I was gone. So many miracles, so little gain.

I could know each one of my disciples by looking into his eyes, but each had eyes that changed by the hour; discontent licked at the edge of their loyalty. Did the great wrath of my Father come from knowing that His chosen people might be more loyal to Satan than to Him?

In my dream on this night, I heard one angel say: "For God so loved the world that He gave His only begotten Son. Whoever believes in Him shall have everlasting life. For God did not send His son to condemn the world but to save it."

How I hoped that the angel spoke truth! For then I would be like a light sent into the world. Yet men seemed to love darkness more than light. I awoke, then, in confusion. For I did not know whether I was here to save the world or to be condemned by the world. Each night I heard a command in my sleep, but the voice was my own; it was there to tell me that I must leave these lands where people waited to touch my garment and go instead among the proud of Jerusalem; I must enter the halls of the Great Temple, even if my days would then be numbered by the fingers of one hand.

I thought of how King Herod had wished to kill me. What a bloody creature was man. The wrath of my enemies was like the heat of hell-fire.

No matter how, I knew that I must lead my followers to

the Great Temple, and suffer what would await me there. And I must do this soon, even if there was no time of year less auspicious. For Passover approached. Jews from all of Judea and Galilee would be coming to Jerusalem. In truth, no one of us Jews could forget that this feast was in memory of our flight from Egypt. To find a new land, we had wandered in the wilderness for forty years. Yet when we were there at last, we thrived. Later, through our sins, we lost it. Now Romans ruled over us. In many years, there had been riots of the Jews against the Romans at the time of Passover, large riots. No time could be more perilous for entering Jerusalem than now. The memory of the glory that had been lost was with all of us.

30

I girded myself to start the trip, but was obliged to wait in Galilee. On no day were my twelve men able to agree on the hour of departure. Even on the morning we were finally about to leave, there was further distraction. Levi had disappeared. We knew that he was drinking wine in alleys with men and women who had not wished to join us. My other apostles were furious: "We remain eleven of twelve," they said. "Let us go."

I said: "If a man has a hundred sheep and one of them goes astray, will the man not go into the mountains to look for the lost one? If he brings back such a sheep, he can rejoice more than over the ninety and nine."

Peter said: "Lord, when I was a boy, I lived with my uncle, who was a shepherd. So was I also a shepherd. And it was not our practice to chase lost sheep. We worked to guard the good ones."

"No," I said. "The Son of Man has come to save what is lost." I heard God sigh. For a thousand years the children of Israel had been His. And in this time so many had been lost. I waited for Levi.

That evening on his return, Levi was distraught. A man who will drink through the day feels near to the anger of others—it is why he drinks. That can be his shield. Was Levi keen to the wrath awaiting us in Jerusalem?

That night I preached for a long time, but it may have been to soothe my own unrest. In truth, I continued to speak even when I saw the light leave the eyes of my apostles. They had heard my words before. Still, there were new faces among us, and I chose to instruct by parable. I had come to learn that all of us, having been created by the Lord, possessed much of the Lord's pride. One learned best when free from the yoke of a preacher. It was better to feel full of His spirit by one's power to solve a riddle.

Therefore, I offered this parable: The Kingdom of Heaven, I told them, was like a man who planted good seed in his field; yet while he slept, his enemy came and sowed bad seed upon it, and these weeds appeared with the good wheat. One of my listeners spoke out: "Should the servants of the householder pull up such weeds?"

"No," I answered. "For you will uproot the wheat as well. Let weeds and good grain grow side by side until the harvest. Then, only then, should you bind the weeds and burn them. And bring the wheat into the house."

But I had another question for myself. How well could the Lord's angels separate good from evil? My journeys had shown me the cunning of men. And priests were more cunning still. What if there was a temple before the gate of heaven that was not unlike a customshouse? Through such gates could slip many an evil person.

Over and over, I had been learning that to my fellow men it mattered less whether they were tall or short, lean or wide, of noble features or ugly, even strong or weak. In one way all were the same: Greed was their guide.

So when Peter said to me, "We have forsaken all and followed you; what shall we have in return?" I replied with another parable, and it was for Peter.

A man hired his laborers for one denarius a day and sent them into his vineyard. As the hours passed, he hired more in the third hour and more again in the sixth and even in the ninth hour.

At the end of the day, he told his steward, "Call the laborers and pay them." Each man, whether from the first hour or the ninth, received one denarius. Since the first supposed that the last would receive less, they complained. But the householder told them, "Did you not agree to work for one denarius? Take what is yours and go. I will give as much to the last man as to you. Let the last be first and the first last."

I was uplifted by the force of my voice and spoke with such strength that the Lord whispered: "Enough! In your speech is the seed of discontent. When you are without Me, the Devil is your companion." And I felt as if the Lord held a thorn to my brow; I no longer knew to whose voice I listened. And I understood that to be the Son of God was not equal to being a Prince of Heaven but instead was my apprenticeship in learning how to speak simply and with wisdom, rather than by bewildering others with the brilliance of one's words; it was to know—most difficult of all—when the Lord was speaking through me and when He was not.

While we waited and worked to keep our spirits together, I had my times of doubt. I had labored in so many ways to reach the hearts of my fellow Jews, good men, even pillars of the community, but so many had wanted nothing to do with me.

It was then I had the longest conversation I would know with Judas. For, in an hour of doubt, I asked him: "Why do they not join me? How can they not wish to enter the Kingdom of Heaven?"

He was ready to tell me. "It is," Judas said, "because you do not understand them. You speak of the end of this world and our entrance into another realm. But a money-lender or a merchant does not want this world to end. He is comfortable with his little triumphs, and he wishes to be able to brood on the losses of his day. So he is at home with everything that proves a little cleaner or a little filthier than it was supposed to be. He lives for the play of chance. That is why he is so pious when he does not play. He suspects that the Lord would never approve of chance, yet here is he, enjoying life to the degree that it is a game and not a serious matter. Except for money. Gold is the center of philosophy for such a person, and salvation is there to contemplate in one's thoughts, but not in one's actions. He could even live with what you say about salvation, except that you ask for too much. You tell him to give everything of himself to it. So you offend him profoundly. You want the world to end in order that glory can come for all of us. Your merchant knows better. A little of this, a little of that, and the Highest One to be revered—at a great distance, of course."

"You speak," I said, "as if you agree with them."

"In my thoughts I am often closer to them than I am to you."

"Then why are you with me?"

"Because many of your sayings are closer to me than any enjoyment I receive by witnessing their games. Having grown up among them, I know what is in their hearts, and I detest them. They continue to believe they are good. They see themselves as rich in charity, in piety, and in loyalty to their people. So I scorn them. They not only tolerate the great distance between the rich and the poor, they increase it."

"Then you are with me?"

"Yes."

"Is it because I know that we cannot reach the Kingdom of Heaven until there are no rich and no poor?"

"Yes."

"Still, you almost speak as if you do not care about entering the Kingdom of Heaven."

"God strike me, but I do not believe in it."

"But you say you are with me. Why, then, are you with me?"

"Can you bear the truth?"

"I am nothing without it."

"The truth, dear Yeshua, is that I do not believe you will ever bring us all to salvation. Yet in the course of saying all that you say, the poor will take courage to feel more equal to the rich. That gives me happiness."

"That alone?"

"I hate the rich. They poison all of us. They are vain, undeserving, and wasteful of the hopes of those who are beneath them. They spend their lives lying to the lowly."

I hardly knew what to reply. He had left me not unhappy. Indeed, I was all but merry. For I could see that he would work for me, and work hard. So, he would help to bring us all to salvation. What a smile of joyous disbelief would be on his face when we entered the gates together.

Only then would he see how all I said came truly from my Father.

I loved Judas. In this hour I loved him more even than I loved Peter. If all my disciples would dare to be as truthful with me as Judas had been, then I could be stronger and accomplish many things.

"If," I now asked, "I ceased to labor—by even a jot or a tittle—for the needs of the poor, would you see less of value in me?"

"I would turn against you. A man who is ready to walk away from the poor by a little is soon ready to depart from them by a lot."

I had to admire this man. Judas had not seen the glory I knew. Yet his beliefs were as powerful to him as were mine to me. Yes, he was more admirable even than Peter, whose faith was as blind as a stone and so could be split by a larger stone.

So too did I know that trouble might arise between Judas and me. For he had none of the accommodation that my Father had given to my heart to make me ready for those trials that could come upon us unforeseen.

I can also say that this conversation with Judas was wondrous for clearing disarray. At last all seemed to be in order. We were ready. I could hardly believe we were ready to set out at last for Jerusalem, but it was a good morning. If none of us were without fear, we were touched by happiness as well. For we had not been enslaved by our fear. Our legs knew their own joy.

Then, and only then, did we truly step out. And in the vigor of our march, many began to believe that in two days when we were close enough to see Jerusalem, the Kingdom of God would appear. The Lord would be among us.

31

All the same, my conversation with Judas must have disturbed me more than I knew, for on the road to Jerusalem I became feverish. As I walked, my limbs ached. At night I had no rest that was without pain. And it was the same on the second morning.

By evening, still a full day's march from Jerusalem, we passed through Jericho and there a rich man named Zacchaeus wished to welcome me. Many were in the throng, however, and he was a small man; therefore he had climbed to the top of a sycamore so that we could see him.

I said: "Zacchaeus, come down. Tonight I will stay at your house."

He received me joyfully. Others said that it was not fitting that I should be the guest of the wealthiest publican in Jericho. But Zacchaeus said: "Lord, now that I know you, half of my goods I will give to the poor."

I was gladdened. For if a rich man could surrender half of his fortune because he believed in me, then there might be walls ready to fall in Jerusalem. I slept well that second night in the house of Zacchaeus.

Next morning as we set out, two sisters of my follower Lazarus came to meet us. I had dined with Lazarus in Capernaum, and he was a good man. Now his two sisters, Mary and Martha, had walked from his house in Bethany to find me, and they said, "Lord, Lazarus is sick, our Lazarus."

And by the way it was said, I knew that he had a sickness unto death.

They wept. As if I were brother to his illness, my fever came back; my night of rest was lost. I had to stay two nights more in Zacchaeus' house, and we were still a full day's march from Jerusalem. When I awoke on the fifth morning of our departure from Galilee, I was well in body but otherwise full of woe, and I said, "Lazarus is dead."

The apostle Thomas was simple, and often uttered what others thought. Now he said aloud, "Let us go to Jerusalem so we can die with him." There was much displeasure at Thomas' remark.

We walked all that day and into the evening before we came to Bethany, where Lazarus lived in a house an hour's walk from the walls of Jerusalem. And I could see many Jews on their way to his home. Indeed, his sister Martha came to meet me, and said, "Lord, if you had been here, my brother would not have died."

I was ready to agree. Nonetheless, I said, "Your brother shall rise again."

Then came Mary, the other sister, and she sat at my feet and was followed by others also weeping, and when they looked at me, I said, "Where have you laid him?"

"Lord, come and see."

How could I know whether God would grant me the power to return him to his sisters? Lazarus had been dead for two days.

Many Jews around me, friends of the dead man, seeing me in anguish, said, "Behold, how he loved Lazarus!"

They led me to a cave with a stone across the entrance. I said, "Take away the stone."

But Martha said: "Lord, who can speak now for his body?"

Yet at my sign they removed the rock from the entrance. I lifted my eyes and cried out, and my voice roared in my throat: "Father, let Lazarus come forth!"

Then I was silent. When the spirit left a man, all that was unclean in his spirit was loosed as well. So I waited for the odor to enter my nose. Indeed, I asked myself:

"How can one raise a dead man from his tomb when all the evil of his past holds him down?"

The Lord must have heard me. I saw the face of Lazarus. I saw him stir.

Again I cried: "Lazarus, come forth." And I heard him answer.

"Oh, Yeshua," said Lazarus, "small creatures speak to me, and they say, 'You are not our master, Lazarus, but our wiping-cloth.' Thus speak the maggots."

I prayed for his misery to cease. And it was then that Lazarus rose in his tomb. I saw him come out of the mouth of the cave and take small steps toward me. These steps were small because he was bound in his winding sheet. His face was also covered. I said to his sisters, "Loosen him, but do not look at him."

Then, in the voice of a man who has dwelt in lands that others have not entered, Lazarus said, "The maggots have left me." His voice was like the small cry of a bird. Yet he was alive.

All who witnessed this fell back in wonder. I knew that the High Priest Caiaphas of the Great Temple, on hearing of this, would gather a council. For more than a few had seen Lazarus rise. So they knew that he stank of the grave. The Pharisees would call me a demon. Why not? I had the power to raise a man who had begun to rot.

I could hear the High Priest. He would declare: "If we leave this Jesus in peace, all Jews will go to him. The Romans will believe that we are in rebellion. Before it is over, the Romans will take all that we have."

I knew that the High Priest Caiaphas might even say, "Is it wrong for one man to die so that the rest will not perish? Is it wrong for this one man to die?"

That day I did not go to Jerusalem but slept in the house of Lazarus. In the morning when I said good-bye, he was weak and his spirit was low. I asked, "Do you believe?" and Lazarus said, "I am frightened of the things I saw when dead. Yet I try to believe." In his weakness, he still took my arm and said, "An angel came to me. All is not heavy."

I said to Lazarus: "Do not fear. You are well favored by the Lord." And to myself I prayed that I was telling the truth.

32

Since I wished my people to feel heartened by our entrance into Jerusalem, I sent forth two of my disciples and told them: "Go into this village before us and ask for a colt on whom no man has ever sat. When you find one, bring him to me. Tell them that the Lord is in need of such an animal."

And they went away and soon found a colt, young and spirited, and led him back. I sat upon this animal, which, until now, had been ignorant of a rider, and I held to its mane. For if I could not subdue such a young beast, how then could I calm the uproar in the hearts of men awaiting me at the Temple?

In time, the colt jumped less and pranced more, and we were able to walk in procession. And I liked the animal. I also felt as hungry as if I might never eat again.

Whereupon, seeing a fig tree that was heavy with leaves, I trotted toward it in order to take my fill. Yet on its branches I found no ripe figs.

Did an ill wind blow toward us? I said to the fig tree, "Let no man eat fruit from you again."

But a weight came upon my heart for cursing the roots of another. "I am the Son of God," I told myself, "yet also a man; by a thread does man live without heedless destruction."

So I also knew that Satan still clung to me. Like a hawk who searches the fields below for one small creature, then swoops for the kill, so had I scourged the tree.

Now the crowd of men and women who walked ahead of me took branches from the palms we passed and strewed them on my path. They sang, "Hosannah! Blessed is he who comes in the name of the Lord. Blessed is the kingdom of our David who comes in the name of the Lord. Hosannah in the highest." And some cried out, "Blessed is the king who comes in the name of the Lord." These people of Jerusalem (and most had not seen me before) were full of favor; in the windows, many waved. Word of our good deeds had come to Jerusalem before us.

Yet I did not forget the fig tree. Its branches would now be bare. Such thoughts made me brood upon the end of the city of Tyre. A thousand years ago it had dwelt in splendor, renowned for its tables of ebony, its emeralds and purple linens, its stalls of honey and balm, its coral and agate and chests of cedar. Yet the sea had washed it all away. Would this yet be said of Jerusalem, as wealthy in this hour as Tyre once had been?

I gazed upon great white buildings with columns so tall that I could not know whether I beheld a temple or a seat of Roman government. I said to myself, "A good name is rather to be chosen than great riches," but the words were too pious (for my heart had leaped at the sight of these riches). So I also said: "The mouth of a strange woman is a deep pit. And a great city is like a strange woman."

Yet I could not scorn Jerusalem. The people of Israel lived with as much magnificence now as in the time of King Solomon, when his palanquin had been made from cedar of Lebanon, its pillars fashioned of silver, its base of gold. The seat of the palanquin was purple and its claws had been wrought by the daughters of Jerusalem. Wondrous was Jerusalem in the time of Solomon, and wondrous was it now.

Yet my followers could hardly share such glory. I saw a Roman noble stop before our procession and stare at our hundreds walking by twos and by threes and fours in the lane. Some were well attired, but most of my people were in plain clothing, or in rags.

I, too, now stared at this throng that belonged to me.

The people of Jerusalem were joining us in large numbers; and I was seeing as many faces as there are aspects of man. Among those who followed were many who could be counted as less than believers but were rather among the curious and the tormented and the cynical, and these last were accompanying us to jeer at the Pharisees and thereby repay them for old rebukes.

Some of these new followers were solemn. So in their eyes shone the hope that I might provide a new piety that weighed upon them less than their old piety, which had turned drab in their hearts from too much repetition of the same prayers. And there were children who looked on all the sights and laughed at the wonder of God's bounty when it came to the faces of people; they were the closest to joy. There were also men with the fearful dissatisfaction of boredom on their brow.

And there were the poor. In their eyes I saw great need, and new hope, and much depth of sorrow; they had been disappointed many times. And I spoke to all, good and evil equally, as if they were one, since changes for the better can occur rapidly at times like these. In a bad man, evil and good can shift more quickly than in a good man; bad men are familiar with their sins and often weary of the struggle to deny remorse.

As the throng increased, so was the colt full of many wicked spirits, but they were young and without the foul odors of more practiced devils. Still, my beast would buck, and I knew it was in his mind to throw me over his head onto the stones of the road. Yet I rode him. He was the colt for me. And for this moment I felt like the master of good and evil.

Only at this moment, however. For as I approached the Temple, I grew solemn with awe. I could not believe I was more than a Jew with a modest trade approaching a great and consecrated edifice. We were coming near to the Temple of Temples, and they had built it on a mount.

Even before I came to it, I remembered that its steps would rise from courtyard to courtyard, facing ever more august chapels and sacred sanctuaries, and there would be one chamber into which only the High Priest could enter and then only on one day of the year. That was the Holy of Holies. I was the Son of God, but I was also the child of my mother and so my respect for the Temple was, with each breath, growing larger than my urge to change all that was within. I shivered when the men and women in front of me, on mounting an incline in the road, began to cheer, and soon I too, on mounting the hill, saw the Temple walls.

But as I took in the sight, so did I also know that the future of this magnificence was in peril. In years to come, enemies would be ready to tear down the walls until nothing would remain but one wall. Hardly a stone would be left to rest upon another. All this would pass unless the priests of the Temple came to understand that my message was from the Lord.

Sitting upon the colt, I wept openly at my first sight on this morning of the Great Temple. It was beautiful, but it was not eternal. And I thought of the words of Amos, who had said: "The houses of ivory shall perish." It was then that I dismounted, and continued on foot.

33

Having climbed the steps of the entrance, I came into the Temple itself. Beyond the first gate was a large court where all could exchange money and goods. How one had to admire the beards of these men of Mammon! They had been curled by a warm iron and were immaculate in their pride. So these moneylenders looked like peacocks. And the priests also looked like peacocks as they moved among them. All was vanity. At home, their tables would be bountiful, while the poor sat in the stinking alleys of the city.

I wrapped silence about me like a holy cloth that others would not dare to touch. I sat alone on a stone bench and looked at how these people cast money into the alms box. Many who were rich cast much. But then came a poor woman, and her shawl was threadbare; she threw in her small coin. My heart leaped.

I called to those disciples who were near and said: "This poor woman has put in more than all the rich. They leave a tithe of their abundance. She gave her living. So she has turned money into a tribute to the Lord. The wealthy give only to impress each other."

I thought of money and how it was an odious beast. It consumed everything offered to it. What slobbering was in such greed! I thought of how the rich are choked with the weight of gold, and their gardens grow no fruit to satisfy them. There is oppression in the perfume of the air, and none of the rich man's blooms bring happiness. For his neighbor is wealthier than himself and his gardens are more beautiful. So are the rich always envious of the next man's gold.

Here, in the outer court of the Temple, surrounded by these moneylenders, I spoke to all, and my voice was my own. I said: "No man can pay allegiance to two masters. For he will cling to the one he needs and, in secret, despise the other. You cannot serve God and Mammon."

Then I heard the Devil speak to me for the first time since I had been with him on the mountain. He said: "Before it is over, the rich will possess you as well. They will put your image on every wall. The alms raised in your name will swell the treasure of mighty churches; men will worship you most when you belong to me as much as to Him. Which is just. For I am His equal." And he laughed. He knew what he would say next:

"Greed is a beast, you say, but note this! Its defecations are weighed in gold. Isn't gold the color of the sun from which all things grow?"

The Lord chose to reply in my other ear: "Everything he says makes sense until it does no longer. He gives this speech to all who catch his eye, and his eye is only for the best, and most beautiful, whom I have fashioned with great hope. He scorns those who are modest but remain with Me."

And this was more than my Father ever said again about Satan, but at this moment it gave little force to my faith. Did my Father speak well of the meek because they were the only ones who remained loyal to Him and to me? How full of chaos was such a thought! I fell prey to a wrath greater than any I had known before.

In the eyes of the moneylenders, greed was as sharp as the point of a spear; the rage of Isaiah came to me. In his words, I cried out: " 'These tables are a pool of vomit. In such filth, nothing is clean!' "

And I overturned each of the tables before me. I threw them over with the money that was on them, and I exulted as the coins gave small cries on striking the stones of the courtyard. Each possessor ran after his lost coins like the swine of Gadarene as they rushed into the sea.

154

Then I knocked over the seats of those who sold doves and I opened the cages. On this commotion of wings the multitude who were with me came forward and cheered at this defiance of usury.

I said: "My house shall be known before all nations as a house of prayer. Whereas you are men of Mammon and have made it a den of thieves."

Indeed it was the truth. Men who sought Mammon were thieves. They were thieves even if they had never stolen a cup of wheat. Their greed stripped virtue from all who would emulate them.

Soon the priests would be speaking of this act in all the sanctuaries within this Great Temple. For the priests, like the moneylenders, also kept their accounts with God separate from their accounts with Mammon. And how quick they were to water all the vines of cupidity that grew on one side of their soul.

34

In the midst of this disorder, I strode among the over-turned tables and said: "Destroy this Temple. In three days I will raise it up."

One of the moneylenders had the courage to speak, a stout old man, but with clear eyes: "It took forty-six years to build what is here. You will restore it in three days?"

Now I had to wonder at what I had said. A folly! There were many in this multitude behind me who were ready to tear down anything that did not belong to them. So the word to destroy, once spoken, could do great harm in days to come. Harsh words live in the dungeon of the heart. They never relent; they never forgive. They are imprisoned.

I knew regret. Here were many buildings of immaculate beauty. If I had been a pilgrim wandering these halls, I would have felt awe for the skill of the builders.

By such thinking did I try to remind myself that I was here to teach, not to destroy.

And I would say that the Lord was still with me. For His rage had been there with mine, had it not? And now who but my Father was telling me to be gentle? I said to my followers, "Respect our Temple. These moneylenders are only the leavings of evil. They can be scrubbed from the stone. Walk with me further into these holy places, and I will teach."

I led them to a quiet garden between two small chapels; there was even a cedar to give shade. Then, as I had foreseen, a delegation came of priests and scribes and many of the elders of Jerusalem. Their spokesman said: "We have been awaiting you. But we do not understand the manner of your arrival. By whose authority do you do these things?"

I answered, "I will ask one question. If you can reply, I will tell you. The baptism of John," I asked, "was it from heaven or of men?"

I knew they would reason as follows: "If we say 'From heaven,' then this Jesus shall say, 'Why, then, did you not believe John?' Yet if we say that John was of men, then all of our devout will say that John had to be a prophet."

Since these priests depended on the allegiance of pious

Jews, and such Jews often feared that their priests were too friendly with the Romans, there was no room for them to admit that John had been a prophet. For then I could have asked: "Why did you not intercede with the Romans and save John?"

So they answered, "We cannot tell."

I said, "Neither shall I tell by what authority I do these things."

A scribe came forward. He approached with such ease that I knew he was from a noble family. His eyes were blue and his brown beard was soft. He smiled as if he were full of affection for me. Indeed, he even said for greeting, "Master"—which, after the disruption I had caused in the courtyard, was a courtesy; if he could not approve of such an act, he would still call me Master. And so, "Master," he said, "we know that you want to teach the way of truth. Therefore I would ask for an answer to this question. It is of weight to us. Would you say it is lawful to give tribute to Caesar? Or shall we not give?"

With all the gentle warmth that this man offered, I also knew that the Devil had minions who were equally fair. If I replied that one must not give tribute to Caesar, which was the reply, I expect, that he awaited, then these Pharisees could tell the Procurator of Jerusalem that I was leading a rebellion against the Romans.

My wit, however, was like an arrow. I said, "Give me a coin."

When they brought it, I asked, "Whose face is on this money?"

The scribe replied, "Caesar's."

I said, "Render to Caesar the things that are Caesar's. And to God the things that belong to God." I was pleased. For I was also telling them that Mammon was a god for the Romans, not the Jews.

I could feel their respect. Now they saw that I not only had the strength to overturn the tables of the moneylenders but the wisdom to avoid a rash reply.

Later, upon reflection, I would also know that my remark had been too clever. While many a church would survive in evil lands by giving homage to Caesar, I was not here to build churches but to bring sinners to salvation. Why, then, had I given that reply? Had God decided on prudence as the better path? Would He now allow churches to grow in the swamps of pride and Mammon?

35

I could see that the scribe who addressed me as Master wanted to continue our discourse. He asked: "What, by your understanding, is the first Commandment of them all?"

I answered: " 'The Lord, our God, is one Lord.' This must be the first Commandment. The second is to love thy neighbor as thyself."

The scribe said: "To love one's neighbor as oneself is more than all burnt offerings and sacrifices."

He was wise in the way he spoke to me. Could he be the Master of the Book in this Great Temple? His manners were as subtle as his well-curled beard. And his speech was as handsome as his appearance. Yet his eyes were pale like the faded blue of the sky when the sky is white. So I did not trust him. Still, I listened as he said: "Here, we are all circumcised. We share a single faith. Many of us in this Temple believe that you have not come here to rend us asunder but to bring us nearer to one another. And this we still believe, even though disruption has followed you like the dust before a storm." He paused to great effect. All among us were now listening to him. "Still," he said, "there are storms that cleanse. So I would ask of you, Master, when will the Kingdom of God be with us?"

As he spoke, I could hear the same two voices that live side by side in many a Pharisee. Their speech is often endowed with good manners, but there is also quiet mockery in their utterance and this is as finely sifted into their courtesies as powder into sand. Nonetheless, I listened. For he was not without some desire to believe that I was the Son of Man. It was possible that the priests who had sent him were also ready to listen. We spoke, therefore, as men who were equal. Only in the second hour did he reveal his knowledge of the scrolls, and thereby began a gentle dispute over the working of cures on the Sabbath.

"Do you recall the verse," he asked, "that says: 'And while the children of Israel were in the wilderness, they found a man that gathered sticks upon the Sabbath day, and they brought him to Moses and Aaron and to all the congregation. But the Lord said to Moses, "The man shall surely be put to death: all the congregation shall stone him." And the congregation took him outside the camp and did stone him and he died.'" The scribe now said, "That was a thousand years ago, and our congregation today would not stone such a man. Yet the principle may remain. You shall not work on the Sabbath."

I replied that I had answered this question many times. "If you circumcise a babe on the Sabbath," I told him, "then you may also lift the scales from the blind and flex the limbs of the halt."

But here he began to speak with such skill that I did not know how or where to interrupt.

He said, "I have been waiting for all of this year to talk with you. For I have thought of your works, Master, and I would say, even as the prophet Samuel said to King Saul: 'Rebellion is the sin of witchcraft.' Contemplate what I have just said. If you come from Him whom you will not declare but wish us to believe is the Lord, why not say as much? For if you refuse to declare yourself, suffering could result from your good deeds. Your cures could appear to us as witchcraft and full of the bright fire of rebellion. We in the Temple fear that fire. We have labored for ten hundred years to learn what is in the Book. Many have died for the five books of the Torah. Yet with the strength of our beliefs we have built the walls of this Temple. We are able to live by the light it provides us. It is the same light that was given to us by the deeds of our martyrs. They died for our scrolls and our laws. So I would remind you, even as it is written in First Maccabees, that King Antiochus, a heathen king, was set over us, and he declared to his whole kingdom that we should now be one people, Jews and gentiles alike. And all were ordered to obey the laws of this new religion even if it was not ours.

"The gentiles agreed. To our shame, many Israelites also consented to a faith that worshipped idols. Indeed, so many accepted these edicts of Antiochus that the only clear measure of a man who was still a good Jew came to be that you could kill him before he would profane the Sabbath.

"Then, King Antiochus commanded us to abstain from circumcising our children. Whoever did not obey would die. Good Israelites had to flee Jerusalem. The priests of King Antiochus then placed swine upon the altar. Whoever was found with the Book was put to death. When soldiers found infants who were circumcised, they killed them. And they hanged the priests who performed the circumcision.

"We learned then," said the scribe, "that our Book could not restrain evil unless all of us gave absolute obedience to the laws of the Book. When we listen, therefore, to what you say, we do not always hear your understanding of the ten hundred years of the Book. Nor do we feel your recognition of the martyrs who died for the Law. Instead, we see that in your haste to serve God, you encourage publicans, sinners, even the uncircumcised. You rush to destroy all that you have learned in all the years of your schooling. Do you not comprehend that blind rejection of the Law is as evil as idolatry?"

I could hear more and more sounds of assent among those who listened. Some of my own people were muttering that he was right. And many had wept as he spoke of the deaths of these martyrs.

I was slow to reply. "Do not think," I told him, "that I am here to deny the Law or the prophets. I have not come to destroy but to fulfill." Here I stopped, and looked into his pale eyes. "Unless the righteousness of my followers exceeds the righteousness of your scribes and Pharisees, we shall not enter the Kingdom of Heaven."

Before he could reply, I added: "All that you say is just if people observe the Book. But they do not. This land of Israel has committed so many great sins that the Lord now looks upon the people of Israel as living in whoredom. Are we not supposed to find a way to save the whore?"

The scribe answered in a tone so light and so full of the wings of confidence that his words danced upon his tongue; in that moment I heard Satan stir in his throat. For he said: "Save the whore? Yes, you will finish by saying to gentiles, a people who are not your people, 'You are my people,' and they will say, 'You are my God.'" And the scribe laughed softly. All the mockery he had mixed into his courtesy settled over me. It was as if he had seen all things evil and wise where I had not. So he knew to a certainty that gentiles were ignorant and worshipped statues whereas he, like other good Pharisees, was of the Chosen.

I did not speak until I could find the words I sought. And then I spoke in Hebrew, even as I had read it in the Book. "From the words of Ezekiel," I said: " 'My sheep were scattered because there is no shepherd, and they became meek to all the beasts of the field when they were scattered. Neither did My shepherds search for My flock, but fed themselves. Behold, I am against the shepherds.' "

"And these shepherds," the scribe answered, "are kin to me? Can it be that this is what you say?"

I was thinking that even a drunken man would know what it was now politic to say. I was lacking in all knowledge of how to offer what would gain the most and offend the least. But then I had no desire to be politic. I wanted these Pharisees to remember my words forever.

"I look," I told the scribe, "to gather my flock from all places, from wherever they have been scattered. So I do not despise those who are uncircumcised or those who are ignorant of the Book."

"Are you saying that you would give a light to the gentiles?" he asked.

"Yes," I said. "That would be for the salvation of all." The scribe was silent; I think he was weary. He had studied the teachings of the great prophets, and they had dreamed of the hour when God would bring salvation to Israel. But it had not come to pass. Was the scribe wondering whether this Galilean and his peasants could know more about salvation than our heroes and prophets, even the kings of the glorious and holy past?

I continued to speak. "The Lord," I said, "has made my mouth a sharp sword. In the shadow of His hand He has hidden me. He has told me: 'Raise up the tribes of Jacob and the strong reserve of Israel.' But He also said: 'I will give you a light to the gentiles in order that you may be My salvation unto all the ends of the earth.'"

To which the scribe said, "Is that not blasphemy?"

I replied, "It is what my Father has said."

On these words he left. With him went many who agreed with his thoughts. A large number. I was alone again with my followers.

36

As the shadows in the great courtyard grew longer with the lowering of the sun, echoes kept returning of all that had been contested between the scribe and myself. Now that I could speak with no one to dispute me, I was more ready to say all that I thought. For I could see that my Father's cause would not prevail unless I was prepared to battle the powers of this Temple, and the great walls of their thought. So I must speak with the mightiest words I could find. Indeed, I could hear the voice of the Lord coming forth from me without errant thoughts of my own.

There were Pharisees still among us, and I began by

saying: "The elders sit in the seat of Moses, and the Great Temple of Jerusalem is their throne. Whatever these elders bid you to observe, observe it. But do not do as they do. For they lay heavy pieties on men's shoulders, yet they will not raise a finger to move our burdens. Rather they look for the chief seats in the synagogues and the uppermost rooms at feasts."

Immediately, the Pharisees stirred. Some began to leave. Yet a few, as if twice fortified, remained to spy upon what I would say further. So I mocked them. I spoke in their voice as if I too were a Pharisee. " 'Look upon me,' " I told them. " 'Am I not prosperous?' " And then said in my own voice, "Do any of you grieve over the bent fingers of the old woman who embroiders the fringe of your prayer shawl?"

Bolder Pharisees began to hoot and others, more timid, chose to leave. But I could also see the faces of those who had lost their houses through the sharp practice of others. "Why," I asked the Pharisees, "did you not feed the widow's children instead of acquiring the house? Slaves of Mammon! If you swear by the gold of the Temple, you will become a debtor to the Lord. Fools! You are blind! You pay tithes of mint and anise and cumin according to the Law and you omit the weightier matters of the Law, which are judgment and mercy and faith. You strain at a gnat and swallow a camel. You clean the outside of the cup and leave the inside full of extortion and excess. You are like sepulchers, beautiful and white, that are full of dead men's bones. You build the tombs of the prophets, yet you are the children of those who killed the prophets."

The Lord had given me these words, and at last I could speak in the brave voice of John the Baptist. I was truly his cousin. "Behold," I said. "I will send prophets to you, and wise men. Some you will kill and some you will crucify; some you will persecute from city to city. And upon you will fall all the righteous blood shed upon the earth until this day.

"O Jerusalem, Jerusalem! You have stoned those who were sent unto you!"

My words fell upon them. All the while, my heart was heavier than the blows they received to their pride. For my words were not false. I knew that these were my people and this was my Temple, and so I must mourn for Israel.

And I could see that it was time to leave. The Pharisees had summoned the Temple Guard.

Yet the throng who still surrounded me had been moved by my words. My people were so ready to protect me that they were like a tempest of whirling sand ready to sting the eyes of any man who interfered with my leaving. Some of the guards held rocks in their hands. But not one was thrown. No man laid hands on my garments. My hour was not come. The guards approached and fell back, approached and fell back, and my eyes told them not to touch my cloth.

In that manner, I departed from the Temple on that first day.

37

Once we were outside the walls, the larger part of this throng now climbed with me to the Mount of Olives. And we were full of joy. I alone could feel the darkness beneath the exaltation.

One after another, disciples came forward to ask: "When are these great things to come? Will we rise at the end of the world?"

I said to them: "The end of the world will come only when I am no longer among you."

As I said this I could feel their pain, and that brought tears to my eyes. For I could see that they loved me more than they did not; I felt again the need to bring them counsel, and so I spoke of the visions in my dream.

I said: "You shall hear of wars and rumors of wars. Nation shall rise against nation and kingdom against kingdom. There will be famine and pestilence and earthquake. All these are but the beginning of sorrow. Others will gather you up to kill you. You shall be hated by all nations for my name's sake. Iniquity will abound. The love of gold will afflict many. But those who endure to the end will be saved. And you shall preach this gospel of the Kingdom to all nations."

In that instant, surrounded by my people, who swayed and cried out at these words, I thought of the minions of the Devil. Was it the Lord's warning? These minions would also come upon the earth, and in my name, and they would be armed with a store of small miracles. Each would claim to be the return of myself. Bottomless deceptions lay before us! I said:

"If any man shall say to you, 'Lo, here is Christ,' or say, 'He is here,' do not believe it. False prophets will arise and show great signs and wonders. If they say, 'Behold, he is in the desert,' do not rush forth into the wasteland. Or if they say, 'He is in the secret chamber,' do not believe it. Only when the lightning comes out of the east and lights up the west will there be the coming of the Son of Man. The sun will be darkened and the moon give no light; the stars will fall from heaven. The power of heaven will be shaken. Only then will the sign of the Son of Man appear and all will see him coming on the clouds of heaven with the great sound of a trumpet. I say to you, this generation shall not pass till all these things are fulfilled. Heaven and earth will pass away, but not my words. Watch, therefore. For you do not know the hour your Lord will come. Yet know this: If the good man of the house had known when the thief would come, he would have watched. He would not have suffered his house to be broken up. Therefore, be ready. For in the hour that you do not expect him, the Son of Man will come.

"He will say: 'Inherit the Kingdom. I was hungry and you gave me meat; I was thirsty and you gave me drink; I was a stranger and you took me in; naked, and you clothed me; I was sick and you visited me; I was in prison and you came to me.' I say to you, whatever you have done to the least of my brethren, you have done it to me. And those who did not shall go to everlasting punishment. But the righteous will have life eternal."

They cheered mightily, as if each of them was certain to be among the righteous. They seemed to believe that the hosannahs of the many were sufficient to do God's work and receive eternal life. How would they ever find their way to the Lord?

Yet I could not mar their confidence. For my words had been powerful. Therefore, I must honor them. If such words owed their force to the eloquence of the Lord, still, I had been their messenger, and it was a mighty message.

38

That night I fasted. The people of Jerusalem who greeted me on my path called me King, but they did not know that my kingdom, should I find it, would be in heaven. They were looking for a monarch who would restore the greatness we had known in Israel under King David.

The dawn was cool, and I, feeling restored, was ready to go again to the Temple and sit beneath a sacred tree. I would teach.

But on the road that went by the Mount of Olives, Pharisees stood in my path, and with them was a woman. They said: "Master, this woman was taken in adultery. She was caught in the very act. The Law commands that she be stoned. What will you say?"

I knew that they would look to accuse me of leniency toward sinners. Therefore I gave my eyes neither to the woman nor to them. "You shalt not commit adultery," I said. "Whoever looks on a woman with lust has committed adultery in his heart." These words were for the young men among them whose eyes reflected their delight that they could stare openly at this woman taken in adultery; I also knew that their thoughts would soon provide idle hands with other forms of delight. To myself, I thought: If thy hand offend thee, cut it off.

This woman before me must have within her every filth and effluence of the Devil's spew, fornication being the most powerful instrument of the Devil. So these Pharisees stood confidently before me, certain that I would find a way to pardon her and thereby admit that I was ready to traffic with whores. But I did no more than stoop down to the earth. And with my finger I wrote in the dust as though I had not heard them.

Their minds were rich with calculation. They knew that to an Essene, unseemly fornication leads directly to the Fire. They would know how much I had learned from the scrolls about the perils of an unclean woman. Indeed, they had read the same scrolls. I remembered what was written of Jezebel in the Second Book of Kings; this Jezebel, a princess, had been thrown down from the high window of a tower, and her blood spattered upon the wall; courtiers rode horses over her and left her underfoot. When the king saw this, he said, "Bury this cursed woman, for she is a king's daughter." But they found no more of her than the skull and the feet and the palms of her hands. So they came and told him and he said, "This is the word of the Lord: 'Dogs shall eat the flesh of Jezebel and the carcass of Jezebel shall be as dung upon the field.' "

Now, I hardly dared to look upon this woman whom the Pharisees had brought to me. Instead, I continued to write with my finger in the sand. If I did not know what I wrote, so I did not let them see it either.

To myself, I whispered from the book of Proverbs: " 'The lips of a strange woman are honey and her mouth is smoother than oil, but the other end is as bitter as wormwood, as sharp as a two-edged sword. Her ways are loose. So do her feet take her down to death, those same feet once so swift in running after mischief.' "

I did not look at her. Peter had come to sit beside me on the ground, and he unrolled the scroll that he carried with him to read when we would rest, and he always carried the scroll, even if he read with great difficulty.

Yet he was close to my thoughts, for he pointed to a passage with his stout finger, twice as thick as one of mine, and in the old Hebrew tongue whispered: "It says: 'On account of a whorish woman is a man brought to a piece of bread.' " When I nodded to go on, he whispered further: " 'An adulterous woman eateth and wipeth her mouth and sayeth, "I have done no wickedness." ' "

I kept nodding in order to keep myself from stealing a look upon this woman. To myself I recited the words of Ezekiel: " 'The Babylonians came to the harlot Aholibah and took her into the bed of love, and they defiled her and she was polluted with them so she discovered her nakedness, yet she did multiply her whoredoms for she doted upon men whose issue is like the issue of horses.' "

Despite myself, I gazed at last upon the woman taken in adultery.

As I feared, she was beautiful. The bones of her face were delicate, and her hair flowed down her back. With art, she had painted her eyes. She was gentle even as her mouth was proud and foolish.

My abhorrence of fornication had filled my years with thoughts of lust. I had suffered the ravages of unspent fury. But now I heard the soft voice of a spirit. Was her angel searching for mercy? I was offered a vision of this woman in the fumes of sin. And with a stranger! Even so, she was a creature of God. She might be near the Lord in ways I could not see, even—could it be?—in the wallow of fornications with strangers. Was she, then, so different from the Son of Man? He too must be close to all strangers. Yes, she could even be close to God all the while that the hands of the Devil embraced her body. Her heart could be one with God even as her body was close to the Devil.

So when these Pharisees, having been as silent and patient as fishermen, now asked me again, saying, "Moses and the Law command us. Such a woman should be stoned. What do you say?" I lifted myself up and spoke not only to my disciples but to the circle of scribes and Pharisees. And this time, I said aloud: "If thy hand offend thee, cut it off." When they looked at me, I told them: "It is better to enter the other life maimed than to have two hands to take into hell." Then I saw fear in their eyes. "If your eye offend thee," I told them, "pluck it out. It is better to enter the Kingdom of God and see only with the eye that is left than have both eyes look into the flames. In hell-fire, the worm that eats at your flesh does not die." I was amazed. I felt cleansed of disturbance toward this woman, and by my own words. So I also said: "He that is without sin among you, let him cast the first stone."

A tumult arose. It was so sudden and of such force that I nearly lost my balance and had to stoop once more and write again in the dust as if I cared more for what my finger could say to the earth than for all of them.

Soon, and with each moment, their fury began to abate. Before long it had fled. Now they were pained by their own misdeeds.

I saw them go away. They left one by one, commencing with the oldest man among them. (He had, perhaps, the most sin to support.) The last to leave was young, and may have been near to innocent. I was alone. Even Peter had departed. Only the woman stood before me.

I could not bring myself to look into her eyes, then I did. In so doing, I still could not see her eyes. Instead, like a dream offered by Satan, I heard a verse from the Song of Songs. "The joints of thy thighs are like jewels, the work of a master's hand" were the words I heard, "and thy navel is like a round goblet." I told myself that I was in the presence of evil angels. For I could find my own evil, and it was rich and dark and begging to be cast forth from me. And these evil angels were so powerful that I knew I must be wary of the beauty of this woman.

So I chose to speak to her in the words of the prophet Ezekiel. I said: " 'Behold your sin. It is written: "I will raise up thy lovers, and they shall come against thee with chariots and wheels, and they shall deal furiously with thee; they shall take away thy nose and ears and thy residue shall be devoured by fire. They shall also strip thee out of thy clothes and take away thy fair jewels. Thus will I make thy lewdness to cease immediately and thy whoredoms be brought out of the land of Egypt, so that thou shall not remember Egypt anymore." ' "

And this harlot, whose eyes were as purple as the last hour of evening, said gently, "I do not wish to lose my nose."

I said, "Woman, where are your accusers? Has no man accused you?"

She said, and her voice was modest, "No man is here to accuse me, Lord."

I said, "Neither do I condemn thee. Go!"

Yet it was not enough. For within this woman remained every echo of her whoredom. So I said: "Where can you go? Are you not bound still to fornication with strangers?"

She replied: "If you do not condemn me, then do not pass judgment. Without the flesh there is no life."

She was vain. She was strong. And I could see that she was wed to the seven powers of the Devil's wrath and to their offspring: the seven demons. So I must attempt to cast out these seven powers and demons. I knew they would come forth slowly. And indeed, when they did come forth, it was one by one, and they clawed at all good spirit between us. Some were sly and some were lewd, and more than one was hideous—seven powers and demons.

The first was Darkness and its demon was treachery. Indeed, I was to realize even as I named each one that I had learned more from Satan than he wished to tell me. So I knew that Desire was the second power and pride would be its demon. And the third was Ignorance, with a huge appetite for the meat of swine, a gluttonous demon. Love of Death was the fourth power and its demon could be no less than the lust to eat another. For nowhere is our knowledge of death closer to us than when devouring flesh from a fellow human. The fifth power sought Whole

Domain and its demon worked to defile all spirit; the good spirit that had come to this woman and myself was much buffeted as this demon came forth. And the sixth power was Excess of Wisdom. Its demon had the urge to steal a soul. Of them all, the last power was the most fearful. It was the Wisdom of Wrath; its demon was the lust to lay waste a city. Such were the seven powers and demons I drew forth from her. Only then could I say: "Go and sin no more." And she left.

Afterward I would learn that her name was Mary and she was from Magdala in Tiberias, a city where many Jews had died in war against the Romans. Their bones now lay under the foundations of the buildings that had been erected by the victors. So this woman Mary Magdalene had committed adultery upon the ground of our martyrs. Yet I did not regret what I had done. For by half she was gentle, and that half belonged to God. Nor did I know that I would see her again. Yet I did.

39

As I continued along the Street of Herodias on the morning of this second day, I was thinking how the street was named after the wife of Herod Antipas, and who could forget that she had ordered the death of John the Baptist? Yet this accursed name, Herodias, had been given to the avenue that leads to the great gate of the Temple.

A blind man now accosted me. Blind from birth, he said. He had known none of the delight of a child's vision. One of my disciples asked: "Master, what sin did the parents of this man commit that he was born blind?"

I replied too quickly: "This man is blind in order that

the works of God can be made manifest to him so soon as he can see. And I will cure him."

When I looked at the eyes of this blind man, however, I saw nothing with which to begin, not even a sightless eye on either side of his nose. There were nothing but two hollows beneath his brow. "I believe," I said to my Father. "Now help my unbelief."

And I spat on the ground and made clay of the spittle and anointed his eyes. Then I said, "Go. Wash in the pool of Siloam," which was the pool beside our path.

He groped his way there, tapping with his stick. When he came back, he could see. I heard him speak to his neighbors, and they said, "Aren't you the one who sat and begged?"

Others replied, "That is the one."

When they asked how he could see, I heard him say, "A man called Jesus anointed me, then told me to wash. Having done so, I can see."

They said, "Where is this Jesus?"

The man said, "I do not know."

On the street, a Pharisee asked him how he had gained his sight, and the man told his story once more.

Now, the Pharisees decided that he had not been blind from birth. So they called to his parents, who were filled with confusion; they could only say, "We know that this is our son and he was born blind, but by what means he now sees or who has opened his eyes, we don't know." Then they said, "Our son is of age. Ask him. He can speak for himself."

Again the Pharisees went up to the man who had been blind and said: "The person who laid clay upon your eyes is a sinner."

The man answered: "Whether he is a sinner, I do not know. But I was sightless and now I see."

"How, then," asked the Pharisees, "did he open your eyes?"

He replied: "I told you and you do not hear. Why would you hear it again? Do you wish to become his disciples?"

The Pharisees said: "We are followers of Moses. But we cannot say where this Jesus came from."

For each moment that this man could see the world as it was, he became bolder. I felt blessed to have given sight to such a fellow. "A marvelous thing," he said now, "that you don't know where this Jesus is from, yet he has opened my eyes. If he did not come from God, could he have done this?"

The Pharisees reviled him. They beat upon him with their fists and said, "Born in sin, and now you teach?" They cast him out.

When my disciples brought him back to me, I said, "I am not only here so that those who are without eyes might see but to teach those who claim to see that they are blind."

And I said this with even more anger than I had known

at the tables of the moneylenders; yes, more. This fury was not in my hands or in my feet; it was not in my voice; it had forced its way into the quiet reaches of my heart. When one of the Pharisees who overheard me say these words now asked, with much mockery, "Am I blind?" I replied, "In your sin you are blind."

The man saw himself as important, and he said, "This Jesus has a devil and is mad." Others argued, "Can a devil open the eyes of a man who was born blind?"

There was much dispute.

Further down the Street of Herodias, an old Pharisee with a kind face, and many lines of wisdom in the twist of his nose and his mouth, came up to me and asked if we might talk. He said, "Many of us who are Jews and devout feel that you did well to overturn the tables of the moneylenders. Your act is a tribute to God. Too few of us are willing to rebuke greed." But, he said, he would like me to understand something that he had not understood when he was young. When I nodded, he began to speak. Indeed, I wished to calm myself before entering the Temple.

"The Lord," he said, "is generous, and created us to be much like Him. Yet though we are in His image, still we know that we do not have His power."

This elder seemed decent to me. I said: "Man may be created in His image, yet there are no miracles in man's hand."

"Yes," he said. "But what of the one who does have miracles? Is he nearer to God? Or has the Devil deluded him? For the Evil One might use his power to do good; that may be within Satan's art. He could have the gift to give sight to a blind man. In that manner he could delude you further, noble Jesus, concerning the source of your miracles. And by that means he could also magnify the delusions you bring to poor Jews."

"What you say," I told him, "is so finely crafted that you could be speaking for the Serpent."

He sighed. He said, "I know you have a noble heart. It speaks from your eyes. I mean only to warn you. Already a few say that you are the Son of God." And he lowered his eyes before so blasphemous a remark. Only then could he speak again: "Some claim that you say it yourself. I pray that no harm will come to you from this. If you meet the High Priest Caiaphas, do not say anything of this nature to him. For if he should hear such words from your mouth, the sacrilege would be beyond measure. Yet for so long as he does not hear it from your mouth but only from others, he will prefer not to listen. For then he will not have to declare that a mortal sacrilege exists. Of such is your safety."

I smiled at him, but I did not know if I could accept his advice.

40

On this second day in the Temple, the numbers who listened to me had multiplied. They stood in the courtyard and were loud and unruly in the force and fever of their prayers, and so there was need to speak on this matter, for if they did not know how to comport themselves in the Lord's house, they would not know how to act when alone.

"Do not be like the hypocrites," I said, "who love to recite pious verses while standing in the synagogues. Instead, pray to your Father in secret. Do not use vain repetition. That deadens the soul. Never be guilty, therefore, of excessive prayer; your Father knows what you need."

But they only wanted to hear of wondrous things, of portents in the heavens that would forewarn them of the end. So once there was calm, I chose to tell of how there would be signs in the sun, the moon, and in the stars, and of how there would be upheaval upon the earth and in the sea: "Men's hearts will fail them for fear. But if they are brave, they shall see the Son of Man coming in a cloud with power and glory. Then you may lift up your heads. For your redemption is near." To myself I said, "Oh, Lord, let my words be true."

I felt as if I had cried out to Him and remained alone. Yet my words were still obliged to do their best to reach into their hearts. For each word might become as valuable as a boat's timber that can keep a man afloat in a sullen sea.

From afar, I could see a priest talking to an officer of the Temple Guard. And one of the lesser priests standing close to me spoke: "By the scrolls it is said that the Messiah shall be from Bethlehem. How, then, can any good thing come out of Nazareth?"

Another said, "No, Jesus is of Bethlehem. Where can you look for a man's nature if not in the land where he was born?"

The priest said: "He is of Galilee. Out of Galilee can arise no Messiah." He nodded his head wisely. He knew. He knew nothing about God, but he could tell you where the Messiah could arise and where he could not.

Listening to this declaration, I told myself: "A man of small mind develops a hard shell so that he can protect his small thoughts." The anger that had reached the center of my heart after the blind man had been mistreated by the Pharisees now came forth in the words I said aloud. "Your fathers killed the prophets," I told them, "and here you build the tombs of the prophets. God will send new prophets, and you will persecute them. You will slay them. So great will be this bloodshed that all the blood of all the prophets that has been shed from the foundations of the world will yet be required of this generation."

When the priest drew back a step, I stepped forward to say more: "All of this has gone on from the blood of Abel to the blood of Zacharias and he perished between the altar and the table."

This priest before me might be small in mind and small in body, but he was as certain as a scorpion of what he knew; he scolded me for offering cures on the Sabbath.

Bereft of patience over this matter, I said: "In you is not the love of God."

How I wished to smite the piety of every Jew who was sharp of practice and narrow of mind. I could have prayed that they find some of the good spirit of those other Jews with whom I had built houses in Nazareth. Those men had been my equals; those men had been my friends.

I said more. I said: "The hour is coming when all that are in the grave shall hear His voice and then they shall come forth, they who have done good and they who have done evil. Then will my judgment be upon all your ancestors." I waited and said again: "Upon all your ancestors."

By these last words I aroused a greater wrath than by anything I said or did on the first day. It burned in these priests and Pharisees. If they suffered in their souls from many sins and lusted after Mammon, still they believed that they would be protected in heaven against their worst acts. For their glorious forebears would intercede. They believed in their ancestors before they believed in God. And more than they believed in God. Their real faith was that these ancient members of their family would carry them across the abyss that separated them from the Lord. And here was I passing judgment on the old and evil deeds of their ancestors. So they closed their ears. They had to protect themselves against giving any kind of audience to the Devil. Tears stood forth in my eyes like sentinels on guard. For I knew that the most powerful of my own people, and their highest priests, could only see me as the messenger of Satan. And I could not believe how deep this wound went into me: I was repugnant to the leaders of my people. Yes! As repugnant as the swine of Gadarene.

So great was their rage that the light of the day turned red before my eyes. It was as if their souls were already in the Fire. Toward such rage I offered no peace. I could not restrain my tongue: "You shall know the truth," I told them, "and only the truth shall make you free." Yet these

Pharisees were proud; from the heights of their self-esteem they offered homage to themselves. So they answered: "We are of the seed of Abraham. We were never in bondage to any man. How then can it be said 'You shall be made free'?"

I answered: "You are Abraham's seed, yet you seek to be rid of me. But I have come to tell you the truth as I have heard it from God."

They answered, "We too have one father, and He is God."

To which I replied: "The Devil is your father."

Was I preparing a furnace to melt iron? Never had I seen Pharisees more provoked. "Now we know," they said, "from whom you come. Do you dare to say that you are greater than our father Abraham?"

"Your father Abraham rejoices to see my day," I told them, "because he knows me. Before Abraham was, I am."

They took up stones to cast at me. No longer could I walk by them as on the first day. Then, some had been ready to hurl a rock, yet could not. I had passed through their ranks. Now one, and soon another, would be bold. And after the first stone, many. So I stepped behind one of my disciples, and he behind others, and we slipped away. Even as they raged in their fire, they still would not be quick to pursue me.

41

Concerned about where I could stay, my disciples chose the house of Simon the leper in Bethany. No one would think of searching there. Yet word of my presence soon went out. While we were at table, a woman came with an offering. It was an alabaster jar of spikenard, which she massaged into my hair. This spikenard was of great worth, as much as three hundred denarii, which is what a poor man earns by his labor over many a month, even a year.

But this spikenard had power over me. Its aroma entered my ears as well as my nose, and I heard the Song of Songs. First came the voice of the Bride. She said: "While the king sat at his table, my spikenard sent forth its fragrance."

Some of my disciples were indignant. One even said, "Why was this ointment not sold by our Master and the money given to the poor? This is waste!" It was Judas who spoke.

I looked at him with disfavor. And he was dark with anger and looked away. The woman who brought the gift was named Mary (the same as my mother, and Mary Magdalene, and the Mary who was Lazarus' sister), and, yes, another Mary whose name I would not forget, for she anointed my feet with the last of the spikenard and wiped my feet with her hair. Nor was I without a sentiment of peace as she gave this homage to my ankles and toes (as if blessing the miles we had walked). Verses came to me from the scroll of the Song of Songs: "Rise up, my fair one, and come away. For, lo, the winter is past, the rain is over, flowers appear on the earth and the time for birds to sing has come." The house was filled with the sweet odor of the ointment.

Judas now asked: "Why was this pomade not sold?"

Others began to complain. They did not speak against me, but they did attack the woman's gift. I said, "Why trouble her? She has left her good work on me." And to Judas I said more: "The poor are with you always," I told him, "and whenever you can, you may do them good. But me you will not have always."

193

Now I was of two minds. The love that had come from this woman's hands had given me a moment of happiness; so at this instant I did not feel like a friend of the poor. Indeed, was I not poor myself? I was certainly living with all the shortness of breath that is one's first companion when there is fear of death. The perfume of the spikenard had been a balm to the loneliness in my belly.

So for the first time, I knew how the rich feel, could understand their need for display. To them, a lavish presentation of their worth was as valuable as their own blood. Thereby, I could also understand that their greed was a potion against foreboding. I had said it was easier to pass a knot through the eye of a needle than for a rich man to enter the Kingdom of Heaven, yet from the other side of my mouth, I had, if only for an instant, been scornful of the poor.

Did I speak with a forked tongue so that I might reach out to all? The perfume of the spikenard was in my nose, and I had an image of beautiful temples. They would be erected for me. I could see how I wanted to be all things to all men. Each could take from me a separate wisdom. Indeed, I thought: Many roads lead to the Lord.

But now I noticed that Judas had left. If he loved me, so did he also love me no longer. Even as he had warned me. And he had gone away into that same night where many now wandered back and forth on the road between Bethany and Jerusalem. And all were wondering about the changes to come.

Disciples came up and said that Judas was speaking ill of me on the street. I was ready to betray the poor, he had said. I was like the others. I had not remained true to my convictions. Yet I was obliged to forgive Judas. For, indeed, had I not scorned the poor? That was true even if I had said the words for one moment, only for one moment. But I had believed the words as I said them. The truth need last no longer than a shaft of lightning in order to be the mightiest truth of all.

42

In my dream it had been foretold that the first day of Passover would be my third day in Jerusalem. On that day the Romans would lay hands on me. And here were my limbs heavy on the morning of this third day. I could not rise. My eyes ached from all I had seen, my ears from all that had been heard; an unholy congestion of spirits was in my chest. Multitudes would be waiting to accompany me to the Temple, more than on the first day, or the second. And I was not ready. I asked myself whether it might not be God's will for me to quit this city so that I might preach by the Sea of Galilee once more. How beautiful was the sun upon the water of the Sea of Galilee.

How many debates had there been during the night among the priests of the Temple? Were they looking to imprison me? Today was the feast of the Passover, and so these priests would hesitate to engage in any deed that might cause riots among the people. Jewish riots would enrage the Romans. The priests could find themselves in much disfavor for failing to protect the peace of the city.

They did not know what to do. Of that, I was certain. But then, I did not know what to do. On this third morning, I could not rouse myself to go to the Temple. If prudence comes to us from God and cowardice from the Devil, the line between cannot always be discerned. Not by a man. On this morning I was no longer the Son of God but only a man. God's voice was weak in my ear; a low fear was in my heart.

By afternoon, the disciples gathered at my bed. "Where shall we go," they asked, "that we may all eat together on the Passover?"

At last, I could begin to act. I said, "Let two of you go into the city and follow the first man you see who is carrying a pitcher of water. Walk with him to his door. Tell him: 'My Master asks for the guest chamber. He would like to eat the Passover here with his disciples.' That good man will show you a large upper room, furnished and prepared. Make it ready for us."

I saw this as clearly as if God had told it to me. And, indeed, the man was soon found. All was as I had said; they made ready the Passover. In the evening, in the dark, I came to that house with my twelve, and we ate.

I remained silent until I took the bread. Then I blessed it and broke it and gave a piece to each of my friends. I recalled the hour when I had broken bread in the desert and five loaves had fed five hundred. In that hour I had lived in the miracle of God's favor, so I said now: "Eat of me, for this is my body." And what I said was true. In death our flesh returns to the earth and from that earth will come grain. I was the Son of God. So I would be present in the grain.

I took the cup, and offered thanks to the Lord, and poured our wine, and recalled other nights when we had drunk together and had felt as if all were one, and things hidden would be revealed. Now, indeed, was much revealed. The wine made me feel near my Father, and I looked upon Him as if He were a great king. Indeed, for these few breaths, my fear of Him was less than my love; I felt close to His long labors. He had sought to bring order to the chaos our people had made. How hard He had worked, and how often He had fallen into rage and sent us into exile for our sins. Yet even as He had scattered us, so had He brought us back. He had sought to forgive us no matter how we had despoiled His Creation. Could I now tell these twelve men at this table that God would come, and soon, to save us? I could not give them such a certainty. For I knew that we Israelites were a scattered and sinful people who would prefer, doubtless, not to be saved but judged. For we were so vain as to believe that we would pass judgment.

Like a soldier loyal yet weary, I said to myself, "O Lord, help my unbelief."

And as I gave them to drink, I said: "This is my blood, which is shed for you and for many."

Whereupon, as I tasted the sorrow of the grapes that had been crushed to make this wine, I told them: "I will drink no more wine until I drink it in the Kingdom of God." The Kingdom of God seemed near.

My apostles stirred. One said: "How can a prophet give his flesh to eat and his blood to drink?"

I said: "Unless you eat the flesh of the Son of Man and drink his blood, you will have no life. But he who will eat my flesh and drink my blood will have eternal life. I will raise him up on the last day. He will dwell in me and I in him."

I heard much muttering. Judas spoke out: "This is a hard saying. Who can hear it?"

I answered: "Have I not chosen you? Are you not my twelve?" And I resisted what I was ready to say next, but then I said it: "And among your twelve, is not one of you a devil?" I said this with certainty. Did I not feel the boundless sorrow of the Lord? I said: "One of you shall betray me. Woe to him. It would have been good if he had never been born."

Such a man must be close to me, as close as my own sins and my own fatigue, for now I felt grief for this man. If he would betray me, his suffering would be greater than mine.

Yet with such thoughts I grew stronger. For strength always came to me when I was enriched by compassion.

I arose from supper and laid aside my garments, and with a loincloth I girded myself. Then I poured water into a basin and began to wash the feet of each disciple.

When I came to Peter, he said: "You shall not wash one foot or the other."

I replied, "If I do not, you can be no part of me."

Peter answered, "Then not only my feet, Lord, but my hands and my head."

Some of their feet were clean, and others' stank of the alleys of Jerusalem; still, I knew whose limbs were brave and which men were ready to flee. So when I was done with bathing all twelve, I said: "In time to come, wash one another's feet as I have washed yours."

But the same thought kept repeating itself: "One of you will betray me." I must even have spoken these words aloud, for now Simon Peter asked, "Lord, who is it?"

I answered: "He is the one to whom I shall give a sop."

And a little later, lowering my bread into the wine, I handed this piece to Judas Iscariot. Much passed between us. And not the least of it was the conversation we had had before we set out for Jerusalem.

Judas' dark eyes grew luminous with the glow of false faith we offer when we wish to hide what we feel. Yet I told myself he was, after all, loyal. Just so much did I wish to believe in him. For I could understand how men could have faith but be faithless. Therefore I said to Judas, "What you will do, do quickly." Even if I did know, I did not, just so much did I love him—so, I said it tenderly. No other man at the table understood; some could have thought I sent him out with a blessing. I had clasped him by the shoulder. And he went out. The night was dark.

I was as moved as if I were ready to walk again upon the water in the Sea of Galilee.

I said, "A new commandment I give to you: Love one another as I have loved you. By this alone shall others know that you are my disciples. For soon I must go, and where I go, you cannot come."

Peter said: "Lord, where do you go?"

I answered: "You cannot follow me now. Only afterward will you be able."

Peter said: "Lord, let me follow now. I will lay down my life for you. I am ready to go with you into prison and into death." He believed it. He was certain that he could never fail me. Even the best of warriors can grow so fond of his deeds that he begins to think he is as large as he wishes to be. But he is not. He can still be blind to himself. I said:

"This day, even on this night, before the cock crows once, thou shalt deny me thrice."

He spoke vehemently: "I will not deny you. Not in any way." And the others spoke the same words.

I said: "Are there swords among us?"

43

When there was no reply, I said, "Let the man who has no sword sell his garment and buy one."

Then they confessed. "Lord, here are two swords," they said, and two of them brought forth short swords, whereupon Peter took one.

I said: "It will be enough." But I wondered. Would twelve legions of angels be enough?

The apostle Thomas now asked: "Lord, how can we know the way?" He was simple, and I had to repeat the same words many times for him to understand. So I said, "I am the way, the truth, and the life. No man comes to the Father except by me." But it was late, and he was not the only one who did not know.

Whereupon Philip said, "Lord, show us the Father."

I told him: "Believe that I am in the Father and the Father is in me."

Now I saw as never before that if they did not believe this, they would be without power to do any works. I told them: "Know only that you must love one another as I have loved you."

Never had I felt more love for them, or more compassion for their weakness. So many perils were waiting. "Know," I said, "that I send you forth as sheep in the midst of wolves. Try then to be as wise as serpents and as harmless as doves. But beware of men. For they will deliver you to their councils and, because of me, they will scourge you and subject you to evil judgment by governors and kings. Yet take no thought of what you must say, for it will be given to you in that hour of trial. It is not you who will speak but the Spirit of your Father." (To that, I could bear witness.)

These words brought fear to many of them. But then, few are ready to seek greater faith by climbing upward, ever upward, against their fear. So I added: "Be not afraid, my friends, of those who kill the body; fear rather Him who has the power to cast you into hell. Fear Him."

Now they might understand at last the fear that lay beneath all other fear: Would they see that death was not the end but the beginning? The joys or the agonies to come would surpass all that they had known before. Had I accomplished this much—that they would no longer keep from looking upon the face of death in the hope that thereby a harsh verdict might be avoided?

I knew that all I had told them was true but for one thing. I had said: "Love one another as I have loved you." Yet my love had been mixed with anger.

So I would tell them what must always be true: "Greater love," I said, "no man can have than this, that he lay down his life for his friend. I tell you again: Love one another. You must."

I spoke as if I had already left them. I believed it. Yet I also believed that I would never leave them. I would be with them tomorrow.

I looked at my apostles, and some were ugly and some were misshapen of body; some were misshapen of nose; the hands of many were thick and broken; the legs of others were crooked. Yet they were not only my followers but my friends. I would love them. "They will persecute me," I said. "They will persecute you. And all these things they will do to you because of me. For if I had not told them of their sins, they would not have had to know that they sinned. Now there is no cloak for their evil."

I heard a roaring in the wilderness, and it was far from my ear even if it was inside my ear. The rage of the Devil was immense. If the Pharisees were now without a cloak for their sin, then the Devil might lose his harvest.

"The time shall come," I said to my people, "when whoever will look to kill you will think that he does service to God. Wars shall be waged in God's name that will profit the Devil."

If I was feeling the sorrow that I might not live to see my disciples for even one more evening, still it was necessary that I say: "Your unhappiness shall turn to joy. For you will come to know yourselves, and then you will see that you are also the sons of the living Father."

I wanted this to be true for now and for eternity, but I also knew that my Father's heart was heavier in this hour than my own. Again, I did not dare to wonder whether I had failed in the larger part of my ministry. Instead, I lifted my eyes and prayed, "Father, give back to me the glory that I had with You before the world was." And it gave me great hope to think that He had been with me from the beginning, and even before the beginning. Might that give me strength in the trials to come?

"Father," I said, "if I am no longer to be in this world, my men are still here and I have given them Your Word. So I pray that You will take them into Yourself and keep them from the evil of others. As You, Father, are in me and I in You, may they also be in Us, and be One with Us. And then the world will believe that You have sent me. The glory which You have given to me I would give to them so that they may be One even as We are One, I in them and You in me."

I could feel the love of God. Such love was like an animal of heavenly beauty. Its eyes glowed in my heart.

As these prayers echoed within my chest, so did I know that I must go again to the Temple even if it was the night of the third day. And I must go with these questions in my heart. If they were heavy, so must I carry them as my burden.

I set out.

44

With every step my legs grew heavier.

When we came to Gethsemane, I said to my disciples, "Sit here. I will pray."

I chose Peter and James and John to come with me and began to mount the small hill to the garden of Gethsemane. It was as if my limbs belonged to another and could hardly stir.

"Keep watch," I said. I hardly knew why, but I said to Peter, "Do not enter into temptation." My soul was sorrowful unto death.

Then I went forward to where they could not see me, and fell to the ground. I prayed that this hour might pass.

I wanted to live in less terror. Sweat was on my brow, and heavy, like drops of blood. I said, "Father, take this cup from me." Yet I knew that the cup of misery would not pass; the pit was bottomless. Suddenly I was afraid of my Father for I was full of pity for myself. I said to Him: "It is not what I will but what You will."

When I made my way down to the three I had left behind, they were sleeping. I said: "Peter, could you not watch for an hour?" By his face, I knew that he was imbued with his own terror and it was as large as mine. For what does a strong man do in the hour of his cowardice but fall into sleep? Yet once again Peter swore loyalty to me , and said he would stand guard. "The spirit indeed is willing," I told him, "but the flesh is weak."

I went off to pray by myself in the garden. And the odor of betrayal was in the flowers. Even in the flowers. When I returned to the other three, they were asleep. Again they had fallen asleep.

I said, "It is enough. The hour is come."

As I spoke, Judas came toward us. With him were Temple Guards and Roman soldiers. He marched straightaway to me and said, "Master, Master," and he kissed me on the mouth. It was then that I knew he loved me too, and more than he could ever have believed.

By no more than half, however, did he love me. His lips were burning with fever. He must have said to the guards: "He whom I will kiss speaks as the Messiah." He could have said no less than that, for they came forward at once to lay hands on me. Peter then drew his sword and struck a servant of the High Priest on his ear. That poor fellow's ear turned raw with blood. I said to this servant, "Suffer no further." And touched his ear and healed him. I asked his name—Malchus. The Roman soldiers were silent and did not come to aid Malchus because he was a Jew, but then they also drew back because I had healed a wound.

I said to the Temple Guards: "Have you come to find a thief?"

Hearing this speech, they seized me, and James and John fled. Even Peter was gone. So were the Roman soldiers.

I suffered these Temple Guards to lead me away.

45

They took me to the house of Caiaphas, the High
Priest, and it was a large house. At the other end of a
long hall, a fire had been kindled, and there, followers of
the High Priest sat together. I could see that Peter, having
stolen after me, now sat among them warming himself by
the fire.

The men who held me put a blindfold over my eyes. And
as soon as that was done, one of these fellows slapped me
on the face. Then several said: "Tell us who struck you.
Prophesy!"

Another, whom I could not see, left his spit on my
cheek.

Then came the priests and the elders and some of the council of the Sanhedrin. I knew false witnesses would accompany them. Soon, two men told the High Priest that I had said, "I will destroy this Temple, and within three days I will build another." Yet they did not agree on whether I had said I would use my own hands or would rebuild the Temple without hands.

Caiaphas, the High Priest, now ordered my blindfold to be removed. He was a tall man, and his white beard was worthy of a prophet. He stood in the midst of the others and asked gently: "Will you reply to my questions?"

I did not answer. My silence must have seemed insolent, for this High Priest Caiaphas then said: "I adjure you by the Living God to tell us whether you are Christ, the Son of God, our Messiah."

He had adjured me. I could not swear a false oath to the High Priest of my people; no, not even if I was the Son of God and thereby, by half, superior to any priest. So I said, "I am what you say." These words might as well have come from the sky. They seemed far away from me even as I said them.

He did not seem surprised. With deliberation, the High Priest tore his robes and said, "We need no witnesses. All of you have heard this blasphemy."

And in ripping his garment Caiaphas had declared to all that I had no claim to be the Son of the Father; no, I was a son of the Jews. This son had committed so great a sacrilege that he, the High Priest, had had to rend his clothes. By the common bond of our people's blood, I was his offspring. Condemned by him, I was now to be mourned as dead.

The guards beat upon me. These words by Caiaphas had removed all fear that I might yet bear witness against mistreatment. So they felt free to beat my face.

I could still see Peter. He remained on a bench at the other end of the hall, and when a servant came up to him and asked, "Were you not one of those who was with Yeshua of Nazareth in the Temple?" Peter said, "I don't understand what you say."

But, at once, he left her and went out onto the porch, even though the night was cold. There, another maid saw him and said: "This is one of them."

Again he denied me. "Woman," he told her, "I do not know him."

A man came up and said to Peter: "Aren't you one of his people? Your speech has the sound of Galilee."

Peter declared: "I do not know this man of whom you speak."

It was then that the cock crowed. It was night, not morning, but the cock crowed. In that moment, Peter recalled what I had said.

He left the porch. He was weeping. He wept. Peter's sorrow passed over to me, but, suddenly, like the point of a lance. He would spend his life offering amends for this hour when he had denied me thrice before the cock crowed once.

The High Priest Caiaphas departed with the elders of the Sanhedrin. And I was thrown into a small dungeon, where I was kept through the night and, unable to sleep, considered what I might do. No matter that Judas had betrayed me; he had also warned me. And now I needed his counsel. It was he, of all my disciples, who had been the wisest in explaining how our priests went about arranging matters with the Romans. So I knew that in the morning, much would depend on the nature of the agreement entered into between Caiaphas and the Procurator of Judea.

Judas had spoken often of these two men and how they kept peace in Jerusalem. Pontius Pilate allowed his soldiers to commit no insolence against the Great Temple, and Caiaphas tolerated no orthodox burial for those Jews who died in attacks upon Roman soldiers.

Thereby they maintained order. The Romans kept belief, as such pagans would, in their own Roman destiny. Whereas the Jews believed in one God, One, more powerful than all pagan gods and demons. On other matters there was much accord between Caiaphas and Pontius Pilate. As Judas had told it to me, the Roman Procurator received gold in secret from the Temple; this made for much difference in the way he treated Jews. In his first year of governing Judea, Pontius Pilate had committed the mistake of displaying the Roman eagle upon the standards of his garrison in the holy city. That was idolatry, and a demonstration commenced against Pontius Pilate. A great number of Jews gathered outside his residence and refused to leave. They were soon encircled by Pilate's legions and ordered to depart or to die. But none of these Jews would take a step. Pilate had to give way. He removed the Roman eagle from the standards of the legions. The Jews had not only been brave but knowing. They had divined that Pilate did not wish to disturb his superiors in Rome by a war at the beginning of his command as Procurator. Now he had ruled over Judea for more than five years, and peace had been preserved, even if he still conducted his affairs with a daily fear of revolt.

Caiaphas had been High Priest for more than ten years. The sum of his agreement with Pontius Pilate was that he also abhorred an uprising. So said Judas, who had seldom been hesitant to show his dissatisfaction with me because I was not willing to lead a revolt. Before the Jews could come to know the brotherhood of man, they must be free of the Romans, Judas had said. That was the only way, he declared to all of us, that the Jews could be free of the shame that kept them apart, some few rich, so many poor, and all subservient to the Romans. Yes, he was furious when I told him that I wished to bring my people to my Father, and that was all I wanted. I had told him this more than once on our journey to Jerusalem, and indeed, I was

innocent of any urge to rebel against the eagle of these pagans. But then, I did not feel subservient to the Romans.
They might hold us in their grip here on earth but they
were as nothing compared to the Kingdom of Heaven.

Could this be cause for hope? That I did not wish to be
a leader of a revolt? Already my limbs had begun to brood
upon their misery, and the bruises on my face were
swollen. This dungeon was blacker than the night.

46

A t dawn, I was taken from the house of Caiaphas and brought to a small chamber near the court of Pontius Pilate. On the way, one of the guards who accompanied me said that Judas had returned the thirty pieces of silver paid to him by the elders.

"Our priests," said the guard, "did not know what to do with this offering. It is not lawful to put blood money into the treasury." So they had refused his thirty pieces of silver. Judas threw down the coins and left.

Then he had hanged himself. Not three hours ago.

How could I comprehend? Of what had Judas repented? Of his lack of belief in my Father? Or his lack of loyalty to me? No, I could not speak. Nor did I dare. For I would have wept. From one side of my heart or the other.

I was taken before Pontius Pilate. He was a small man with a sharp nose and sharp shoulders. His knees were also sharp, as if he had climbed to many a position by the quickness of his mind and his joints. And indeed it is rare to find a man with a sharp nose who is stupid. Nothing of benevolence came from him, but I could see that he was wary and might not wish my death. Rather, he looked upon me as if I were a strong wind that bore no good omen.

Of the priests who now appeared he asked: "What accusation do you make against this man?"

They said: "He is, sir, a malefactor and is trying to pervert our nation."

"Then take him away," said Pilate. "Judge him according to your law."

They answered: "It is not lawful for us to put a man to death." That was true. The power of execution was reserved for the Romans. On those words, therefore, Pontius Pilate left his hall of judgment to take counsel, and when he came back, he asked more questions of these priests, and they said that I had forbidden everyone to give tribute to Caesar and that I called myself a king.

Whereupon Pilate asked: "Do you call yourself the King of the Jews?"

I answered, "Did others say so?"

Pilate answered, "Am I a Jew? Your priests have brought you here. What have you done?"

"My kingdom is not of this world," I answered.

He looked at me then with attention and yet with amusement. For he saw the bruises on my face. He asked, "Are you nonetheless a king?"

"In one way only am I a king. I can bear witness to the truth."

Pilate said: "What is truth?" He might be without belief, but he was not without a tongue. He said, "Where there is truth, there will be no peace. Where peace abides, you will find no truth."

From the party of the High Priest now came a small sound of dissent. If pious Jews knew nothing else, they knew what was truth. And on this morning their truth was that I should be condemned by the Romans.

Having heard their unhappy responses, Pilate asked again: "Yes, what is truth?" And answered the question himself. "In property is truth," he said. "In land is truth, especially in the ownership of it. And in the law of the land is the most truth. Since you are a Galilean, you are under Herod's jurisdiction, not mine. For he is the king of Samaria and Idumea and Galilee as appointed by Rome. Indeed, Herod is not only in Jerusalem this morning but is visiting my court. He has spoken of you and desires to meet you, having heard many things. Perhaps he hopes to see a miracle." Pontius Pilate smiled. "Can your miracles be performed in the court of the gentiles? The gods of the gentiles, after all, may have more domain in this place than the god of the Jews."

So I was taken across many courtyards of his palace and into the chambers of Herod Antipas. He was fat, and he did not say much. He was distracted by a beautiful woman who sat at his table. Yet when his soldiers smiled at seeing me, for by now my robe was filthy, Herod ordered another to be brought, worthy of a king. Or, as he amended it, a robe fit at least for the officers of a king. And he had it put upon me.

Then he said: "Since you are in Jerusalem, you are in the jurisdiction of Pontius Pilate." These words pleased him. I could see that he would send me back to Pontius Pilate. He wanted nothing to do with any cousin of the prophet if others were there to dispose of such a fellow. Instead, Herod Antipas remarked: "Since you are a Galilean and come from lands I oversee, I will send you back to Pontius Pilate in this manner, properly dressed." And his eyes were small and buried far in his head. How they must have hidden from the bloody sight of the head of John the Baptist. He hardly looked at me. His hand was on the woman.

The guards led me through the palace back to Pontius Pilate, and there before him stood Caiaphas, who looked as if he, too, had not slept in peace.

Pilate was speaking: "You have sent this man to me as

one who perverts your people. Yet I have found no fault in him that corresponds to your accusation that he breeds revolt against Romans. Nor does Herod find such fault. Look, he has sent him back in a robe of purple. Therefore I will chastise this man, then release him. When you ask that I condemn a man to death, it can be done only if he is a grievous malefactor. Death, when all is said, is a grievous punishment."

I could see that this was not a contest in logic but a game. For Caiaphas showed no discontent. He merely smiled ruefully, as if he knew that the price of Roman justice would not be small today. Pontius Pilate might be ready to put me to death, but only at his price.

Now Pilate said: "I will condemn this man if you insist, but is it necessary? Today is one of the days of your feast. By our law, which is here in accord with your law, it is agreed that I am to release one Jew who has been in prison during your Passover. Will you let me release to you this King of the Jews?"

The priests of the Temple made a show of looking all around them for an answer: I could see that none of my people were here, but then my people were poor or, if rich, timid; nearly all were unlettered and afraid of the Romans. Whereas here were many elders of the Temple and scribes and Pharisees and rich townspeople. These were the men surrounding the priests. So I understood (and much too late!) that the voice of a multitude is a high wind: It can do much damage in its passage, but will leave no more than the spoil it has strewn behind.

When Pilate asked: "Whom do I release?" this gathering, loyal to the priests, answered, "Barabbas." And I had heard already of that man. Barabbas was a prisoner who had killed a Roman soldier.

Pilate smiled. Roman law might be Roman law, but it would cost the Temple a goodly sum to free a Jew who had killed a Roman soldier. Caiaphas also smiled more widely than before, as if to say, "I have the strength to bear this burden."

So Pilate said: "What, then, should I do with a man who is called Christ?"

Some shouted: "Let him be crucified!" That was enough to arouse the interest of Pontius Pilate. "Why should Jesus be crucified?" he asked. "What great evil has he done?"

Indeed, he seemed curious. If they were looking for a crucifixion, why had these Jews not chosen Barabbas? Since Romans believe that good judgments serve public order, they would decry murder; to them it is a deed worthy of the sentence of death, and even in the harshest form. But blasphemy is merely an insult to a god; it can be placated by prayer or by shifting one's worship to another god. As these Romans looked upon it, prophets were no more to be esteemed than rich merchants. You do not kill a dishonest merchant; you fine him. Pontius Pilate may even have been surprised by how many cried back:

"Crucify him! Crucify this Jesus!" And so he saw that for the Jews, virtue was not to be found in land but in the punishment of sin.

Pilate called for a bowl of water and washed his hands. Then he said: "I am innocent of the blood of this person." Even I knew this was his way of accepting their decision.

Caiaphas and his people replied: "Let the blood of this man be on us, and on our children." They were sincere. Their belief was deep enough to take a vow upon their children, whereas Pilate would only take a gift.

I wanted to cry out: "Do not take such a vow! My blood will be not only upon your children but upon your children's children, and all of their descendants. Catastrophe beyond catastrophe will follow." Yet I had to be silent before the certitude of these people, who were also my people.

The Roman soldiers took me into their common room and stripped me of all but a loincloth. Then they covered me with that purple robe fit for a king's officer. They plaited a crown of thorns and placed it on my head and handed me the stout stalk of a reed for my right hand. It would be my scepter.

Now they bowed before me, touching their knees to the ground, and cried out: "Hail, King of the Jews."

Whereupon they rose and spit in my eyes and whipped me upon the head. They were Romans, and crude.

They forced the wreath onto my forehead, pressing

down on the thorns until the blood began to run from my brow. And that trickle of blood felt like the white worm of death crawling down my flesh.

Soon enough the robe was taken away. In my nakedness, they returned the old garment to me. And it felt as tender upon my skin as the hand of the Lord upon a newborn babe.

47

As we came out of the palace of Pontius Pilate, there was a man, Simon by name, a Cyrene, who was chosen to bear my cross. Now, I knew why they had jeered at me when I had stood before them with no clothes. For I was no longer the carpenter who worked each day in Galilee, and with vigor. Naked, what was left to me now but my bones? And they laughed and again they called me King of the Jews.

We came to a place called Golgotha, where we were followed by many women who lamented after me. Some of my followers had returned, and these women were first among them and they kept crying out as if they were feeling my pain before I would suffer it.

I had not sought to save the world through the efforts of women. Only through the strivings of men. Now, if my throat was dry, this much I could say aloud: "Daughters of Jerusalem, weep not for me but for your children. The days are coming in which they shall say, 'Blessed are the barren, for the wombs that never bore and the breasts which never gave suck.'"

I thought of the fig tree I had cursed and added silently: For that, too, I ask forgiveness. And I thought of my days as a carpenter, when I used to pray that a good piece of wood not split.

In the crowd, I saw my mother. Soon I would be torn from her. Now, and too late, I understood her love. I was a gift from the Lord, and so, in her awe of me, she had contended with all I did. For to live constantly in awe is like not knowing one's own child. But in this hour, she was in great pain for me. I belonged to my mother again. Beside her was standing my disciple Timothy, so I said to Mary, "Do not cry. I am return-ing to my Father. Woman, behold thy son." And to him I said, "Here is your mother." He nodded. He would take her into his home. Of all my disciples, he was the one to take care of her, for he had a patient and generous heart.

Not far from my mother, I saw Mary Magdalene. I said to her (and it was at odds with what I had said to the daughters of Jerusalem, but still I whispered): "Take hope. Have children. For God has forgiven you."

On the hill of Golgotha there would be with me two thieves. Indeed, they had already been nailed to their crosses. Now they were raised. Even as they screamed in pain, Pontius Pilate approached. He looked at the sign tied around my neck, which said: "Jesus of Nazareth, King of the Jews." Most of the priests from the Temple had chosen not to remain, but of those still present, one said to Pilate, "That should not read 'King of the Jews.' Whatever he said means little. One does not become a king by saying it."

Pilate replied: "What is written is written."

Again, I could understand his purpose. If, in years to come, they would speak of me as having been the King of the Jews, then Pontius Pilate would be known as one of the first to agree. After all, he had allowed me to wear such a title to my death. And if I were not to be seen in the future as any kind of king, then he would be admired for his power of ridicule. By one road or the other, he was a good Roman. It took a quick mind to benefit from two conclusions when they were opposite to each other. I was learning how these Romans had conquered so much of the world, but I was learning too late.

The soldiers led me to a cross lying on the ground. The wood was crude, and nailed together with slovenly blows of the hammer. It offended me that it had been built so poorly, but in any case they removed my robe and made me lie down upon the cross and stretch out my arms.

I took a breath and the morning was dark. Again I was alone and naked but for my loincloth.

48

They drove a spike into each of my wrists and another spike through each of my feet. I did not cry out. But I saw the heavens divide. Within my skull, light glared at me until I knew the colors of the rainbow; my soul was luminous with pain.

They raised the cross from the ground, and it was as if I climbed higher and into greater pain. This pain traveled across a space as vast as the seas. I swooned. When I opened my eyes, it was to see Roman soldiers kneeling on the ground beneath my feet. They were arguing how to divide my garment so that there would be a piece of cloth for each of them. But my old robe was without a seam, being woven from one end to the other. Therefore they decided: "Let us cast lots. It is only good for one."

The soldier who won took up the garment, and I remembered the woman who had been cured of an issue of blood by touching my robe. Now it hung from the arm of the soldier. And the cloth was as limp as the discarded skin of a snake.

Beside me someone groaned. Another man replied. I looked at the two thieves: One was by my right hand; the other, on the left. Below us, a man said: "He saved many; why can he not save himself?" Another said: "Since he is the Son of God, where is his Father?"

The thief to my right side now spoke: "If you are Christ, save me!"

I told myself: This man thinks only of his own life. He is a criminal. But the other thief said: "Lord, remember my face when entering your Kingdom."

I told him: "Today, you shall be with me in paradise."

I could not know if I believed my words, or whether the thief would hear them. My voice was less than a whisper. Even now, in the hour of my need, I was true to one poor habit—I kept offering my promises to all.

It was still morning, but darkness had come over the land; it was dark. Within myself, I recited a verse from the Psalms: "My bones are burned with heat; my bowels boil; my skin is black."

Yet as Job had passed from fever into that chill which is

worse than fever, so I shivered in my loincloth. From out of my nakedness, I said aloud: "The face of the deep is frozen." I could not hear God's reply. When I said, "I thirst," one of the soldiers came forward to offer me vinegar. When I refused, for vinegar is worse than thirst, he said: "King of the Jews, why don't you come down from the cross?"

And I remembered what was written in the Second Book of Kings: "Hath he not sent me to the men who sit on the wall, that they may eat their own dung and drink of their own piss?"

I cried out to my Father, "Will You allow not one miracle in this hour?"

When my Father replied, it was like a voice from the whirlwind. He said in my ear, and He was louder than my pain: "Would you annul My judgment?"

I said: "Not while breath is in me."

But my torment remained. Agony was written on the sky. And pain came down to me like lightning. Pain surged up to me like lava. I prayed again to my Father: "One miracle," I asked.

If my Father did not hear me, then I was no longer the Son of God. How awful to be no more than a man. I cried out, "My Lord, hast Thou forsaken me?"

There was no answer. Only the echo of my cry. I saw the Garden of Eden and remembered the Lord's words to Adam: "Of every tree in the Garden you may eat freely, but from the Tree of the Knowledge of Good and Evil, you shall not eat."

Let my Father's voice strike Golgotha and His thunder become as loud as His voice, but pain had driven me to believe what one must not believe.

God was my Father, but I had to ask: Is He possessed of all Powers? Or is He not? Like Eve, I wanted knowledge of good and evil. Even as I asked if the Lord was all-powerful, I heard my own answer: God, my father, was one god. But there were others. If I had failed Him, so had He failed me. Such was now my knowledge of good and evil. Was it for that reason that I was on the cross?

One of the soldiers took a sponge, filled it with vinegar, and forced it between my lips. He jeered at me.

The taste was so vile that I cried out with the last of the heavenly rage left to me, and I looked upon the face of the Roman soldier who had squeezed this vinegar into my mouth. "I have a prayer," he said. "I wish you were Barabbas. I would torture you. I would wipe my filth upon your face."

At that moment the Devil spoke. "Join me," he said, and his voice was in my ear. "I will introduce this bully of a Roman to a few humiliations I can lay upon men. There is no pleasure greater than revenge itself. And," said the Devil, "I will bring you down from the cross."

It was a temptation. Only one thought kept me from assent. Tears hot as fire stood in my eyes at this thought, for it told me that I must say no to Satan. Yet I knew. By these hours I had lived on the cross, I knew. My Father was only doing what He could do. Even as I had done what I could do. So He was truly my Father. Like all Fathers He had many sore troubles, and some had little to do with His son. Had His efforts for me been so great that now He was exhausted? Even as I had been too heavy to walk in the Garden of Gethsemane.

By the aid of such a thought, as sobering as the presence of death itself, so did the Devil's voice withdraw from my ear. And I returned to the world where I lay on the cross.

Yet now I felt less pain. For I had learned that I did not wish to die with a curse in my heart. I had told my disciples: "He who kills you will believe he is performing service for God," and those words came back to me—a comfort in this extremity. I said, "My Lord, they do not see. They came into the world empty and they will depart from the world empty. Meanwhile, they are drunk. Forgive them. They know not what they do."

The strength of my life passed from me and entered the Spirit. I had time only to say, "It is finished." Then I died. And it is true that I died before they put the spear in my side. Blood and water ran out of my side to mark the end of morning. I saw a white light that shone like the brilliance of heaven, but it was far away. My last thought was of the faces of the poor and how they were beautiful to me, and I hoped it would be true, as all my followers would soon begin to say, that I had died for them on the cross.

49

In the lifetime of those who came after me, pious scrolls were written by those who had known me. Gospels were set down by those who had not. (And they were more pious!) These later scribes—now they were called Christians—had heard of my journeys. They added much. They spoke of angels arising at my death. Others gave a description of lightning that broke the great lintel of the Temple that day. They told of rocks splitting apart and graves opening. They claimed that when the spikes were pulled from my wrists and my ankles, and I was set on the ground, the earth began to shudder. Some even wrote how prophets arose, came out of their tombs, and marched into the holy city offering their appearance to many. And the people said: "Truly, this was the Son of God."

Many of those who had been near me were given to exaggeration; not one had believed in the Son or in the Father sufficiently to say no more than the truth, which, as you have seen, was much. Therefore I, like Daniel, would now seal my gospel and hope that its truth is everlasting.

Yet I cannot. For I must speak of what was said after I was gone. I have been told many tales, and a few are close to events I knew. Indeed, it is true that I rose on the third day. Yet my disciples added fables to their accounts. When a man sees a wonder, Satan will enter his tale and multiply the wonder.

This much is true: On the afternoon of my death a man named Joseph of Arimathea, who was one of my followers and a rich man, went in secret to Pontius Pilate and asked for permission to take my body. For a good sum, Pilate agreed. Thereupon, Joseph of Arimathea dressed the body which had once been mine, and with him was a man named Nicodemus. They brought a mixture of myrrh and aloes, about a hundredpound weight, and washed me and wound me with new clothes and put me in a linen shroud together with their spices, which is how we Jews bury the dead. And near where I had been crucified was a garden with a sepulchre, newly hewn from the rock, and this was the place that Joseph of Arimathea had prepared for himself. But such was his generosity that he laid me there.

So I was placed in a rich man's tomb. And they rolled a large stone before the door, and left.

Now, Caiaphas and some of his priests had sombre thoughts. They could not be certain that what they had done was wise. By the night of my death, many good Jews were beating their breasts in the streets of Jerusalem and saying, "Our sins will bring woe upon us." The priests of Caiaphas were now concerned that no ill consequences befall their people and themselves. So on the morning after my death, they came back to Pilate and told him that I had said to many: "After three days, I will rise again." They asked the Procurator to safeguard the sepulchre for the same three days. "Otherwise," they said, "disciples of Jesus could steal him away at night, then say to the people, 'He is risen from the dead.' Should that happen, every disruption will multiply."

Pilate said to them, "Keep your own watch." For they would not pay him what he asked. Pilate then said, "I am clean of this man's blood. It is all your doing." Those words they took as a threat, and so they decided to pay him after all. Pilate gave them Petronius the centurion and his Roman soldiers to stand guard by the tomb. And these Romans put seven seals against the large stone at the entrance and set their watch.

There are some who say that there was an earthquake and the angel of the Lord descended from heaven to roll back the stone from the door. Since the raiment of this angel was as white as snow, the guards fled.

Others say that very early on the morning of the third day, even as death can bring together the harlot and the woman who is virtuous, so did Mary Magdalene come to the sepulchre, where she met Mary my mother. And they agreed to perform proper rites for me. But now that they were there, who would roll away the stone?

Yet when they looked, they saw that the tomb was open. They could enter. Inside, they met a young man who wore a long white garment, and he said: "You seek Jesus of Nazareth, but he is risen. Tell his disciples that he goes before you into Galilee and there you shall see him."

This may be close to the truth. For I know that I rose on the third day. And I also recall that I left the sepulchre to wander through the city and the countryside, and there came an hour when I appeared among my disciples. I said to them: "Why are you sad?" And they did not recognize me. They thought I was a stranger in Jerusalem and did not know what had happened. They even said to me, "Our sorrow is for Jesus of Nazareth, who was a mighty prophet. But our rulers have crucified him."

I said to them: "Behold my hands and my feet!" And Thomas looked and, seeing the holes, he asked to feel them (which is why he is known to this day as Doubting Thomas). But the sight of these wounds allowed them to believe. Soon, all who were there began to say that I had been received in heaven and was seated on the right hand of God. In any case, I had by then wandered away and they could no longer see me. All the same, my disciples went forth and preached that the Lord was with them. And they came at last to believe that they had the power to cast out devils. They spoke with new tongues, and when they laid hands on the sick, a few recovered.

But the Jews were much divided by my death. Many went forth with my disciples and became new followers, calling themselves Christian; others remained close to the Temple and argued among themselves for a hundred years over whether I was or was not the Messiah.

The rich among them, and the pious, prevailed; how could the Messiah be a poor man with a crude accent? God would not allow it!

Still, it must also be said that many of those who now call themselves Christian are rich and pious themselves, and are no better, I fear, than the Pharisees. Indeed, they are often greater in their hypocrisy than those who condemned me then.

There are many churches in my name and in the name of my apostles. The greatest and holiest is named after Peter; it is a place of great splendor in Rome. Nowhere can be found more gold.

God and Mammon still grapple for the hearts of all men and all women. As yet, since the contest remains so equal, neither the Lord nor Satan can triumph. I remain on the right hand of God, and look for greater wisdom than I had before, and I think of many with love. My mother is much honored. Many churches are named for her, perhaps more than for me. And she is pleased with her son.

My Father, however, does not often speak to me. Nonetheless, I honor Him. Surely He sends forth as much love as He can offer, but His love is not without limit. For His wars with the Devil grow worse. Great battles have been lost. In the last century of this second millennium were holocausts, conflagrations, and plagues worse than any that had come before.

Yet it is believed by most that God gained a great victory through me. And it may be that the Devil was not clever enough to comprehend the extent of my Father's wisdom. For my Father knew how to recover from debacle and disaster. Some fifty or more years after my death, the Gospel According to John was composed, and the work of this John (unknown to me) may have been illumined by my Father, because John's words proved unforgettable. They said: "God so loved the world that He gave His only begotten son that whosoever believed in him should not perish but have eternal life." So powerful is the force of this message that no other prophet has ever been followed by as many who were ready to die in his name. Of course, I was not only a prophet but His son.

Nonetheless, the truth is more valuable even than the heavens. Thereby, let it be understood: My Father may not have vanquished the Devil. Less than forty years after I died on the cross, a million Jews were killed in a war against Rome. The Great Temple was left with no more than one wall. Still, the Lord proved as cunning as Satan. Indeed, He understood men and women better than did the Devil. For my Father saw how to gain much from defeat by calling it victory. Now, in these days, many Christians believe that all has been won for them. They believe it was already won before they were born. They believe that this victory belongs to them because of my suffering on the cross. Thereby does my Father still find much purpose for me. It is even by way of my blessing that the Lord sends what love He can muster down to that creature who is man and that other creature who is woman, and I try to remain the source of love that is tender.

Yet I must also remind myself of Pontius Pilate, who said that in peace there was no truth, and in truth, no peace. For that reason I do not bring peace but a sword. I would wage war on all that makes us less than we ought to be, less generous. I would not want the Devil to convince me that the quarries of our greed are a noble pit and he is the spirit of freedom. But then, who but Satan would wish to tell us that our way should be easy? For love is not the sure path that will take us to our good end, but is instead the reward we receive at the end of the hard road that is our life and the days of our life. So I think often of the hope that is hidden in the faces of the poor. Then from the depth of my sorrow wells up an immutable compassion, and I find the will to live again and rejoice.

END

ACKNOWLEDGMENTS

I would like to give an acknowledgment to my wife, Norris; to my assistant, Judith McNally; to my friends Michael Lennon and Robert Lucid; to Veronica Windholz; and to James and Gaynell Davis, who all offered signal contributions to this work. And not least, to Jason Epstein, Joy de Menil, and Andrew Wylie.

ABOUT THE TYPE

The text of this book was set in Aster, designed by Francesco Simoncini in 1958. Aster is a round, legible face of even weight, and was planned by the designer for the text setting of newspapers and books.